Kandy Shepherd swapped a career as a magazine editor for a life writing romance. She lives on a small farm in the Blue Mountains near Sydney, Australia, with her husband, daughter and lots of pets. She believes in love at first sight and real-life romance—they worked for her! Kandy loves to hear from her readers. Visit her at kandyshepherd.com.

Books by Kandy Shepherd

Harlequin Romance

Sydney Brides

Gift-Wrapped in Her Wedding Dress
Crown Prince's Chosen Bride
The Bridesmaid's Baby Bump

A Diamond in Her Stocking
From Paradise...to Pregnant!
Hired by the Brooding Billionaire
Greek Tycoon's Mistletoe Proposal
Conveniently Wed to the Greek
Stranded with Her Greek Tycoon
Best Man and the Runaway Bride
Second Chance with the Single Dad

Visit the Author Profile page
at Harlequin.com for more titles.

S0-ABB-186

To Elizabeth Lhuede, good friend and my first critique partner on my romance writing journey. She's still there with wise and informed feedback, not only on writing but also on the quirks of human behavior. Thank you, Elizabeth!

Praise for
Kandy Shepherd

CHAPTER ONE

NATALIA KNEW SHE should have eyes only for her friends, the bride and groom, as the deliriously happy couple exchanged vows in the grounds of a waterfront mansion on Sydney Harbour. The correct etiquette and protocol for every possible social occasion had been drummed into her since birth. *'You must always follow the rules, Natalia.'* She could almost hear the commanding tones of her parents. But, although she knew it was an impolite no-no, she could not help her gaze from straying to the tall, darkly handsome guest on the opposite side of the informal garden aisle. He was hot. Unbelievably hot.

What *was* it about Australia? Since she'd arrived in Sydney, five days previously, she'd never seen so many good-looking men. But none had triggered her interest like this one.

She'd noticed him as soon as the guests had started arriving—broad-shouldered and imposing, black hair, wearing an immaculately tailored charcoal tuxedo. Spanish? Middle Eastern? Greek? It was difficult to tell from this distance. She'd sneaked more than a few surreptitious glances since, each lingering longer than the last.

This time he must have sensed her gaze on him because he turned to meet it.

Mortified, she froze. For a long second her eyes connected with his and he smiled, teeth dazzling white against olive skin, dark brows raised in acknowledgment. She flushed and quickly averted her gaze, looking down with feigned interest at the Order of Service card in her hand.

Despite her reputation in the gossip pages, Natalia wasn't a flirt, or a ruthless breaker of men's hearts. In fact she could be cursedly shy when she encountered an attractive man. But there was something about this fellow wedding guest that made her want to smile right back boldly. To flutter her eyelashes and let him know how drawn she was to him.

Instead she twisted the card between her fingers, determined not to look up again. Breach of protocol aside, she'd been warned to stay right under the radar so as not to take attention away from the bride and groom by her presence. That *didn't* mean conducting a public, across-the-aisle flirtation with a handsome stranger.

But then she remembered with a giddying rush of excitement that she was here incognito and in disguise. Those constricting rules need not apply to her alter ego. *She could do whatever she liked.*

No one but a select few were aware that she was Princess Natalia of Montovia, second in line to the throne of a small European kingdom, notorious for her six refusals of proposals of marriage from royal suitors and her seeming determination to stay single.

Her presence could draw unwanted media attention. The press intrusion was here, even in faraway Australia. Her brother Tristan, the Crown Prince, had married a Sydney girl, and every move they made was newsworthy. The condition of Natalia being allowed to accept the invitation to this wedding, where her brother was a groomsman and his wife a bridesmaid, was that she—Princess Heartbreaker—stayed out of the gossip pages.

So Natalia had chosen a full-on disguise for her stay in Sydney. Her shoulder-length dark brown hair had been straightened, lengthened with extensions and lightened to a honey-blonde that complemented her creamy skin. She'd tried coloured contact lenses to darken her blue eyes, but they'd hurt so she'd abandoned them. Her exclusive designer clothes had been replaced with a wardrobe purchased from a smart high street chain—she'd picked outfits that a regular, non-royal twenty-seven-year-old woman would wear—and her priceless jewellery was locked in a safe back home at the palace, save for a single pair of diamond ear studs.

So far, to her delight, no one had guessed her

secret. And the more she knew she was getting away with her disguise, the bolder she'd become at testing it.

Not-Princess Natalia—at this moment not bound by her kingdom's rules—lifted her eyes and turned back to face the handsome guest, to find him still looking at her. She smiled, sure and confident, though she was racked with nerves inside. His answering grin made her flush grow warmer and awareness shimmer through her body.

Natalia had a sense that he was assessing her, in a subtle yet thorough way. Daringly, she did the same to him. On longer examination he was every bit as hot as he had appeared at first glance. Her smile danced at the corners of her mouth and she angled her shoulders towards him, scarcely aware that she was doing so. His grin widened and he nodded almost imperceptibly in acknowledgment of their silent exchange.

Her heart started beating in excitement. What next? Should she—?

At that moment the celebrant declared Eliza and Jake man and wife, and the newlyweds exchanged their first married kiss, to the accompaniment of happy sighs and cheers from their assembled family and friends. Natalia automatically turned towards the flowered arch where her friends were kissing, and watched as the couple started their march back down the grassy aisle. The bride was flaunting a neat baby bump, which was cause for great celebration.

'Don't you want to have children?'

Natalia's mother, the Queen, had asked that question—for what must have been the zillionth time since Natalia had turned eighteen—as she'd reluctantly said farewell to her only daughter.

Of course she did. And she wasn't averse to marriage. But she wasn't going to couple up with a man she didn't love just so she could have children and ensure further heirs to the throne. Besides, at twenty-seven she wasn't panicking. She simply hadn't met a man who thrilled her, either before or after the lifting of the edict that royals had to marry royals. In theory, she could now marry anyone she liked. That was if she ever fell in love.

Was it because of the men or herself that she'd never felt that giddying elation? Maybe she had to face up to the fact she wasn't a 'falling in love' person. Perhaps she didn't have it in her to trust someone enough to fall in love. Certainly there were very few examples of happy relationships in her family to inspire her.

She believed with all her heart that Tristan and Gemma's happy marriage would last the distance, but it was an exception. Her other brother's arranged marriage had been trumpeted as a 'love match', but his wife had turned out to be cold-hearted and greedy. Her selfishness had, in fact, contributed to her husband's death. And then there were the King and Queen... As a teenager she'd been devastated to discover her parents' marriage was a hypocritical sham.

But this wedding here in Sydney was the real deal, and it gave Natalia a skerrick of hope that true love could be found—among non-royals, anyway.

The bride shone her a special smile as she passed between the rows of white chairs set out on the lawn of the mansion. Eliza was one of the few here who knew her real identity. Eliza and Jake were friends of her brother Tristan. And Eliza and Tristan's wife, Gemma, along with their friend Andie, who was married to the best man, Dominic, ran Sydney's most successful party planning business, Party Queens.

Gemma now lived in Montovia and participated in the business from a distance. Her new sister-in-law had become a close friend, and Natalia had met the other two Party Queens on their visits to Montovia.

She had been thrilled to receive an invitation to Eliza and Jake's wedding. Not just because Eliza was a friend, but also because she'd wanted to see Sydney—the place where Tristan had met his wife Gemma, the place where he had spent a glorious few weeks as an anonymous tourist. She'd wanted a rare chance to be anonymous too. To be herself. Possibly even to find herself.

After the rest of the bridal party had passed by, she looked over to the handsome stranger with bated breath, only to see an empty chair.

Finn was caught up in a swell of well-wishers, all rushing past him to congratulate the bride and groom. As they thronged around him he lost sight of the beautiful woman across the aisle. By the time he'd elbowed past the other guests he could only see the back of her head as she hugged Eliza, her long blonde hair glinting golden in the afternoon sun. Then he himself got caught up in conversation with the best man, Dominic.

Weddings tended to bring out the grouch in Finn. He was what people delighted in calling 'an eligible bachelor'. He'd even, to his horror, been included in a well-publicised list of 'Bachelor Millionaires'—but he was a private person and loathed being in the spotlight. A wedding seemed to bring out matchmaking efforts in even the most unlikely of his friends and acquaintances, all keen to introduce him to potential spouses in whom he had no interest whatsoever. Marriage was not on the cards for him. Not in the foreseeable future.

Thankfully, property developer Dominic wanted to talk business, not potential brides, but real estate was the last thing on Finn's mind. He ground his teeth in frustration at the effort of being polite when all he ached to do was find an opportunity to see her again—the gorgeous sexy woman in the dark pink dress that hugged her curvaceous form. He had to see if she'd felt the same zing of attraction. That instant awareness that hadn't struck him for a long, long time.

After Dominic went on his way Finn politely but impatiently brushed off a stranger who wanted to gush about how romantic the wedding was and headed for the veranda of the beautiful old Kirribilli house where the reception was being held. He had one thing on his mind—to find that lovely woman before some other guy did.

Where was he? Natalia searched the throng of guests, the women wearing a rainbow of dresses, the men in shades of grey and black. No hot guy.

Eliza had ridden up the makeshift aisle on a pony, and a cluster of people had gathered to admire the little mare tethered under the shade cast by the late-afternoon shadow of a towering fig tree. Hot guy wasn't there either.

Natalia was five-foot-five in bare feet. Her stilettos gave her some height advantage over the crowd, but not enough to locate him.

She headed for the mansion where the meal was to be served. Then climbed the short flight of wide, sandstone steps to a veranda that gave a view of the garden to the harbour beyond.

From her new vantage point she scanned the throng in the garden below. *Dignity, Natalia, dignity.* A princess did not chase after a man—no matter how devastatingly attractive she found him.

She rested her hands lightly on the veranda railing, so any onlooker would think she had paused to admire the view of the Opera House with its white sails on the opposite shore of the harbour. Then she tensed at the sudden awareness that tingled along her spine. All her senses seemed to scream an alert.

Him.

Slowly she turned around. The hot guy stood behind her, framed by the arched sandstone windows of the mansion. Just steps away he looked even more handsome than at first glance. Sculpted cheekbones, and his eyes… Not the dark brown she had expected but lighter—hazel, perhaps. A sensuous mouth that lifted in a half smile.

He held a flute of champagne in each hand, tiny bubbles floating rapidly upwards like the excitement rising in her. He stepped forward and offered her a glass. 'I snagged these from a waiter heading out to the garden.'

That voice! Deep, resonant, husky… The tone sent shivers through her. Her hands felt suddenly clammy with nerves. But it would be most un-princess-like behaviour to wipe them down the sides of her dress. She reached out for the flute, hoping it wouldn't slide out of her grip. The movement brought her closer to him, so close that she caught his scent—spicy, fresh, *male*—so potent it caused her pulse to quicken.

She wanted to close her eyes and breathe him in. Instead she took a breath to steady herself. 'Thank you,' she murmured.

'Most welcome. You're a friend of the groom?' he said.

How did he know that? Panic seized her voice, choking any possible reply.

'You were on the groom's side of the aisle,' he prompted.

'Yes. Yes, of course. Jake is a family friend.'

Tristan, Jake and Dominic had been friends for years, having met on the ski slopes of Montovia long before their Party Queens spouses had come along. Jake had been Tristan's best man at his wedding to Gemma.

But Natalia didn't want any questions about their connection. 'You, of course, were on the bride's side.'

'I went to university with Eliza. Since then I've done business with her party planning company.'

'I met her quite recently,' Natalia said.

Eliza had been one of Gemma's bridesmaids

at her brother's spectacular wedding in the grand cathedral the previous year. Just the kind of wedding her parents intended for *her*. Dread squeezed her at the very thought. Marriage Montovian royal-style seemed more like a trap than a gateway to happy-ever-after.

'Eliza's lovely, and she seems so happy.'

'Yeah,' he said. 'And Jake's a good guy.'

Natalia had devised a cover story for her alter ego, but it didn't go very deep. Stalling, she gulped some champagne as she tried to keep the details straight in her mind.

Hot Guy seemed to have no such hesitation. He transferred his glass to his left hand and offered his right. 'Finn O'Neill,' he said, by way of introduction.

Natalie stared at him, spluttered over her champagne, and coughed. Then she quickly recovered herself. 'I'm sorry, I—'

'You were startled by my name? Don't worry. You're not the first and I'd lay a hefty bet you won't be the last. Irish father; Chinese grandfather and Italian grandmother on my mother's side.'

So that was where those exotic good looks came from. 'No. I…er…' She started a polite fib, then thought better of it. To conceal her identity she was being forced to fib. No need to do so unnecessarily. 'Yes, I was surprised. Your name doesn't match your looks. Not like the Irish guys I've met, that is.'

'I'm a fine example of Australia's multicultural population,' he said lightly.

He was a fine example of a male.

Before she could dig herself in any further, she took his hand in a firm shake. 'Natalie Gerard,' she said. Natalie seemed a less memorable name than Natalia; Gerard was her father the King's name. She actually didn't *have* a surname—she was simply known as Natalia, Princess of Montovia.

'By the sound of your accent, you're English,' he said.

'Er…yes,' she said.

She didn't like to lie. But she'd promised her family not to blow her cover to anyone, in case of leaks to the media. Princess Heartbreaker in disguise at a wedding would be the kind of thing they liked to pounce on. So lie she must—though she'd rather think of it as tactical evasion.

Thank heaven for the English-born tutor married to a Montovian woman who had taught her perfectly accented English from the time she'd started to speak her first words. She also spoke impeccable German, French and Italian, with passable Spanish. So for today she would be English.

'Do you live here?' Finn asked.

She shook her head. 'Sadly I'm just visiting on vacation. I wish it were longer. Sydney is fabulous.'

'Spring is a good time to visit,' he said.

'Yes, it is,' she said. 'I'm loving it here.'

Just plain Natalie, a tourist, had spent the last three days riding the ferries, visiting the beaches, taking in a concert at the Opera House. She'd revelled in her freedom and anonymity—even though her two bodyguards were always at a discreet distance. As they were here now, masquerading as waiters.

Perhaps Finn had snagged the champagne from one of them. She was so used to the constant presence of household staff and bodyguards she scarcely noticed their presence.

'Where do you live in England?' Finn asked.

'London,' she said.

The royal family had a house in Mayfair, where she'd lived for a while when she was studying. Until the paparazzi had snapped her staggering out of a nightclub after one too many cocktails and she'd been recalled in disgrace to the palace before she'd been able to finish her degree in architecture.

'Whereabouts in London?' he said. 'I visit there quite often.'

No need to get too specific… Natalia chose to

answer the second part of his question instead. 'What takes you to London?'

'My import/export business,' he said.

Which could, she thought, mean anything.

'What do *you* do?' he said.

Nothing she could share with him. Being Princess of Montovia was pretty much a full-time role. She wasn't allowed to be employed—rather had thrown herself into charity work.

Her main occupation was with the charity she'd started, which auctioned worn-once designer clothes and accessories donated by her and others in her circle to benefit her particular interest—the promotion of education for girls wherever they lived in the world.

Her online fashion parades and auctions had taken off way beyond anything she'd anticipated. Donations of fashion items now came from wealthy aristocrats and celebrities from all over Europe. Bids came from all around the world. The administration was undertaken by volunteers, so profits went straight to where they were needed. She was proud of what she had achieved through her own initiative. But that had nothing to do with Natalie Gerard.

The fact was, she'd been destined for a strategic marriage rather than a career. Especially after the tragic accident nearly three years ago that had robbed Montovia of her older brother Carl and his family, and pushed her up to second in line to the throne after Tristan, now Crown Prince.

Her life had changed radically after the tragedy, with her parents now obsessed with maintaining the succession to the throne. She'd had to work within their restrictions, not wanting to add to their intense grief in mourning their son and two-year-old grandson, still reeling from her own grief, not to mention the outpouring of grief throughout the country.

But she was beginning to weary of doing everything by the royal rules. She wanted her own life.

She couldn't share any of that with Finn. Instead she aimed for impartial chit-chat. 'I work in fashion,' she said.

That wasn't too much of a stretch of the truth. Organising her high-end fashion auctions *was* a job, if not a paid one.

'Retail or wholesale?'

'Retail.'

Her role often required several changes of formal clothing a day. That involved a lot of shopping in the fashion capitals of Europe. In fact, that had kicked off her idea for the auctions—she and other people in the public eye were expected by fashion-watchers to appear at functions in a different outfit each time. That meant expensive garments were often only worn once or twice.

'You fit the part.'

His eyes lit with admiration as he looked at her simple sheath dress in a deep rose-pink overlaid with lace. It wasn't silk, but it was a very good knock-off of a French designer whose couture originals took up considerable hanging space in her apartment-sized humidity-controlled closet back at the palace before they were moved on to auction.

'Thank you,' she said, inordinately pleased at the compliment. 'What do you import and export?' she asked, deflecting his attention from her.

'High-end foods and liquor,' he said. 'It takes me all around the world.'

She nodded. 'Hence your work with Party Queens?'

'Exactly,' he said.

She finished her champagne at the same time he did, then placed her glass on the wide veranda railing. Someone would be along to pick it up.

But Finn reached for it. 'I'll put that glass somewhere safer,' he said.

Mistake, she thought as he took the glasses and placed them on a table just inside the doorway. Regular girl Natalie would *not* be used to household staff picking up after her.

Finn was back within seconds. 'Tell me, Natalie, are you here with a partner?'

He glanced at the bare fingers of her left hand—without realising he did so, she thought. She did the same to him. No rings there either.

'No partner,' she said.

'Good,' he said, with a decisiveness that thrilled her.

'Either here at the wedding or in my life.'

'Me neither,' he said. 'Single. Never married.'

Her spine tingled at this less than subtle trumpeting of his single status. She was single and available too. For today.

Maybe for tonight.

'Likewise,' she said.

This handsome, handsome man must be thirtyish. How had such a catch evaded matrimony?

'D'you think they've put us at the singles table for the meal?' he asked.

'I have no idea,' she said. 'I… I hope so.'

'If they haven't I'll switch every place card in the room to make sure we're seated together.'

She laughed. 'Seriously?'

'Absolutely. Why wouldn't I want to sit with the most beautiful woman at the wedding?'

She laughed again. 'You flatter me.'

He was suddenly very serious. 'There's no flattery. I noticed you as soon as you walked across the grass to take your seat. I couldn't keep my eyes off you.'

She could act coy, not admit that she'd noticed him too, flirt a little, play hard to get… But she'd never met a man like him. Never felt that instant tug of attraction. And time was in very short supply.

'I noticed you too,' she said simply.

For a long moment she looked up into his eyes—up close a surprising sea-green—and he looked down into hers. His gaze was serious, intent, totally focused on her. The air between them shimmered with possibility. Her heart set up a furious beating. She felt giddy with the awareness that she could be on the edge of something momentous, something life-changing. He frowned as if puzzled. Did he feel it too?

'Natalie, I—'

But before he could say any more Gemma came up the steps, Tristan hovering solicitously behind her. Her sister-in-law smiled politely, as if Natalia were just another guest, although her eyes gleamed with the knowledge of their shared secret. Tristan's nod gave his sister a subtle warning. *Be careful.* As if she needed it. She was only too aware of her duty.

Duty. Duty. Duty. It had governed her life from the moment she was born. Duty to her family, to the Crown, to her country. What about her duty to *herself*? *Her* needs, *her* wants, *her* happiness? She was twenty-seven years old and she'd toed the line for too long. If she wanted to flirt with the most gorgeous man she had met in a long time—perhaps ever—she darn well would, and duty be damned.

She took a step closer to Finn. Smiled up at him as Tristan went past. The rigid set of her brother's shoulders was the only sign that he had noticed her provocative gesture. But Finn mistook her smile for amusement.

'I know,' he said. 'It isn't every day you go to a wedding where the groomsman is a prince and the bridesmaid a princess and everyone is pretending they're regular folk like you or me. That's despite the security detail both out on the road and down on the water to keep the media scrum at bay.'

'Bizarre, isn't it?' she said lightly.

In fact, it was rare that she went to a wedding where the bride and groom *weren't* royalty or high-ranking aristocracy. This wedding between people without rank was somewhat of a novelty.

'Bizarre, but kinda fun,' Finn said. 'When else would our paths cross so closely with royalty? Even if the Prince is from some obscure kingdom no one has ever heard of.'

Obscure? Natalia was about to huff in defence of her country. Montovia might be small, in both land mass and population, but it was wealthy, influential and punched above its weight on matters of state. But for today she was just plain Natalie—

not Princess Natalia. And she wanted to enjoy the company of this very appealing Aussie guy without getting into any kind of debate that might give the game away.

'A prince is a prince, I guess, wherever he hails from,' she said.

'And a princess always adds a certain glamour to an occasion,' Finn said drily.

'Indeed,' she said.

A smile twitched at the corners of her mouth. *If only he knew.*

'Talking of fun…let's go inside and swap those place cards if we need to,' she said.

'Yes, ma'am,' he said.

Startled, she almost corrected him. *Ma'am* was a term of address reserved for her mother, the Queen, not her. But of course he was only using the word generically. She really had to stay on the alert if she were to successfully keep up the act.

She went to tuck her hand into his arm but decided against it. If she touched him—even the slightest touch—she wasn't sure how she'd react. She'd only known Finn O'Neill for a matter of minutes but she already knew she wanted him.

He could be the one.

CHAPTER TWO

FINN FOLLOWED NATALIE along the veranda towards the ballroom of the sandstone mansion where the formal part of the wedding reception would shortly take place. He couldn't take his eyes off her shapely swaying hips. How could she walk so surely and confidently in those sky-high heels? Maybe it was the sexy shoes that gave her bottom that enticing little wiggle. Maybe—

She stopped abruptly, so that they collided.

'Sorry,' he said automatically. Although he wasn't sorry at all to be suddenly in such close proximity to this enchanting woman.

'No need to apologise,' she said, not moving away from him.

Her blue eyes glinted with mischief and her lush mouth tilted on the edge of laughter. He was close enough to catch her perfume…sweet, enticing and heady. She didn't seem in the slightest bit disconcerted by the sudden intimacy. Whereas he was overwhelmed by a rush of sensual awareness. He ached to be closer to her. *To kiss her.*

He took a step back from temptation, cleared his throat. 'Why did you stop?'

'I believe this is the room where the meal is to be served,' she said in a conspiratorial tone, gesturing to where wide French doors had been flung open to the veranda. She glanced furtively around her in an exaggerated dramatic way.

'Coast is clear,' he said, amused by her playfulness.

Drinks were still being served in the garden. They had time before the other guests would flood into the ballroom.

He followed her as she tiptoed with dramatic exaggeration to the threshold of the room. Over her shoulder he could see circular tables set up for a formal meal, with a rectangular bridal party table up top. All elegantly decorated with the Party Queens trademark flair.

'No one in there,' Natalie whispered.

'Okay. Commence Operation Place Card Swap. We'll make a dash for it. You—'

She put her finger up against her lips. 'Shh... We have to be covert here. No bride likes her arrangements to be tampered with. We can't be caught. You go in—I'll guard the door.'

Finn found Natalie's place card first and filched it from its silver card holder. Then he searched for the place that had been assigned to him. As anticipated, he had not been seated anywhere near Natalie—four tables away, on the other side of the room, in fact.

Predictably, Eliza had placed him near Prue, a friend of hers from university, who was an attractive enough girl but who didn't interest him in the slightest—in spite of Eliza's matchmaking efforts. There was also the fact that Prue often played fast and loose with the truth, and if there was one thing Finn loathed it was a liar. Yet Eliza persisted.

That was the trouble with weddings. There was some kind of myth—promulgated by women—that a wedding was the perfect place to meet a life partner. Love being in the air and presumably contagious. As a result, weddings brought out their worst matchmaking instincts. As if, at the age of thirty-two, the combined efforts of his Italian, Chinese and Irish families to try and get him to settle down weren't enough, without his friends getting in on the act.

Marriage didn't interest him. Not now. He'd lost the urge when his first serious love had broken both their engagement and his heart. No one he'd met since had made him want to change his mind. Besides, he was in the midst of such a rapid expansion of his business, opening to exciting new markets, and he did not want the distraction of a serious relationship. International trade could be tumultuous. He had to be on top of his game.

He removed Prue's place card and deftly replaced it with the one that spelled out *Natalie Gerard*. Things were definitely looking up. Now he'd be sitting next to the only woman at the wedding who held any appeal for him. The only woman who had sparked his interest in a long time.

'I'll put this place card where yours came from and no one will be any the wiser,' he explained to his accomplice, who had now stepped cautiously into the room.

'Except Eliza,' Natalie said.

'Who I doubt will even notice the swap,' he said.

Natalie, for all her bravado, seemed unexpectedly hesitant. A slight frown creased her forehead. 'Is it really the right thing to do?'

'To sit next to me? Without a doubt.'

'I mean to mess up the seating plan.'

'A minor infringement of the wedding planner's rulebook,' he said.

'An infringement all the same. I... I usually play by the rules.' She averted her gaze, looked down at the pointy toes of her shoes.

'Perhaps it's time to live dangerously?' he said.

Her frown deepened. 'I'm not sure I know how to do that.'

'Live dangerously?'

She looked back up to face him. 'Yes,' she said uncertainly. The mischievous glint in her blue eyes had dimmed to something distressingly subdued.

'Then let me be your tutor.'

'In the art of living dangerously?' she said.

'Exactly,' he said.

She sighed. 'You can't imagine how tempting that sounds.'

The edge to her voice surprised him. 'Don't you ever give in to temptation?' he challenged.

Her smile returned, slow and thoughtful, with a sensuous twist of her lips. 'It depends who's doing the tempting.'

She was so tempting. Finn held up his hand. 'Consider the position of your tutor in Living Dangerously for Beginners to be officially filled,' he said.

She laughed, low and throaty. 'I hope you find me an apt student.'

He hoped so too.

'We'll start by finishing the place card swap. Why don't you do it? Your first "living danger-ously" challenge.'

It would be a step towards others infinitely more interesting.

'That's not so dangerous,' she said, with a dismissive sweep of her perfectly manicured hand.

There was a touch of arrogance to her gesture that surprised and intrigued him. 'You think so? The sun is setting and I think I can hear people coming up the steps to the veranda. You'll have to be quick if you don't want to be caught in the act and bring down the wrath of the bride on your head.'

Any hint of haughtiness gone, Natalie made a sound somewhere between a squeal and a giggle that he found delightful. Without another word he held out Prue's place card.

Natalie snatched it from him. 'Mission accepted,' she said.

He watched as she quickly click-clacked on her high heels—hips swaying—to the table where she'd originally been seated and slid the card into place. When she returned she gave him a triumphant high five.

'Mission accomplished.'

'Well done. Now I won't have to find excuses all evening to visit you at your table.'

'And I won't need to take any opportunity to seek you out at yours.'

She coloured, high on her cheekbones, in a blush that seemed at odds with her provocative words.

'Would you have done that?' he asked. 'Seriously?'

'Of course,' she said. 'You are by far the most attractive man here.'

She seemed such an accomplished flirt, and yet her blush deepened and her eyelashes fluttered as she voiced the compliment.

'Thank you,' he said.

Considering the men of the bridal party were all good-looking billionaires—one a prince—

Finn could only be flattered. And gratified that the instant attraction wasn't only on his side. He wasn't a fanciful man, but insinuating itself into his mind was a thought, wispy and insubstantial but growing in vigour, that this—*she*—was somehow meant to be.

'You know I intend to monopolise you all evening?'

'Monopolise me all you want,' she said slowly.

She was looking up at him with what he could only read as invitation, although there was an endearing uncertainty there too.

'You won't be able to escape me.'

'Do you see me running?' she murmured.

Her gaze met his for a long moment, and he wasn't sure of the message in those extraordinary blue eyes.

Then she smiled. 'Talking of escape—thank you for rescuing me from the table of people I don't know at all but who I suspect are Eliza's elderly relatives.'

'Don't speak too soon. We don't know who we've got sitting at my table.'

'Yes, we do,' she said.

He frowned. 'How did you—?'

She spoke over him. 'Each other. And that's all that counts.'

The words hung between them, seemingly escalating their flirtation to a higher and more exciting level of connection. Finn felt a buzz of excitement and anticipation.

'Quite right. Your first exercise in living dangerously has paid off. I don't care who else is on the table so long as your place card is still next to mine.'

Attending this wedding solo was more duty than pleasure, fond as he was of Eliza, and keen as he was to keep up his contact with Party Queens. But he wasn't one for wasting time on social chit-chat with strangers he might never see again.

An evening spent in the enchanting Natalie's company was a different matter altogether. Enjoying the pleasure of her company was now at the forefront of his mind.

Finn was about to tell her so, but there was a sudden burst of chatter from outside on the veranda. 'The other guests are starting to arrive. We shouldn't be seen in here.'

Natalia's eyes widened in alarm. 'We've got time to get out through that connecting door.'

He reached out his hand and pulled her towards him. 'Let's go before they realise we've been up to no good. Then we'll march back in with the other guests and take our places at the table.'

'Innocent of any crime of swapping seats,' she said.

Not so innocent were his thoughts of where he hoped the evening might lead.

* * *

Natalie couldn't have borne it if she had been forced to sit on the other side of the room from Finn. She didn't want to waste a minute of this wedding away from him.

Tristan had probably had a hand in where she had been placed in the seating arrangements and might not be pleased at the switch. Too bad. Princess Natalia might have to sit dutifully where she was directed—not so just plain Natalie. She was going to grab this chance to be with Finn, no matter if she got dressed down for it later.

Tristan took his role of Crown Prince seriously. That meant protecting her. Since the loss of their brother, she and Tristan had looked out for each other. But sometimes she had to remind him that she didn't take kindly to being bossed around by her brother.

With Finn holding her hand, she made it safely out of the room without detection. Just the casual touch of his hand clasping hers sent shivers of anticipation through her. Never, ever had she felt this kind of thrill.

She was pleased when he didn't drop the connection after they'd made it to safety. Then, together, they strolled casually back into the ballroom alongside a group of other guests.

Each time she looked up to catch his eye she had to suppress a laugh, and saw that he did too.

She felt like a naughty schoolgirl. Although in the private all-girls school she had attended there hadn't been anyone as handsome as Finn to get into mischief with.

Their surreptitious work had paid off—the swapped name cards were still in place. Finn was hers for the duration of the celebration. She was scarcely able to believe that this gorgeous man was real and seemed to want to be with her as much as she did with him.

'We did it,' he said in a low undertone after they'd taken their seats at the table. 'I caught Eliza glaring at me, but there's nothing she can do about where we're sitting from where she is, way up there on the bridal table.'

'Clever us,' Natalia said, holding his gaze and revelling in the warmth of his smile.

So this is what it's like to be really attracted to a man.

Her thoughts were filled with nothing but him. *Insta lust.* That was what her English-speaking friends called the sudden overwhelming desire to be close to a man. But it wasn't just a physical attraction. She liked Finn more than she could have imagined she could like someone in such a short space of time. Yes, she ached to touch him, to feel his smooth olive skin under her fingers, and wondered what it would be like to kiss him. But she also wanted to talk with him, listen to him, laugh with him, find out all she could about him.

She had never felt like this about a man before. Certainly never for any of the six men of noble birth she had rejected as potential husbands. Not even for the boy she'd had a crush on as a teenager in London.

It hadn't just been her being caught out at a nightclub that had seen her recalled home to Montovia. She'd also been seen kissing Danny—a fellow student definitely not on the palace-approved list. It had hurt when she hadn't heard from him again, and part of her heart had shut down, never to recover. It hadn't been until much later that she'd discovered he'd been paid off by the palace to disappear from her life.

Her family's betrayal had added a whole new level of hurt.

Back then, the law that forbade her and her brothers from marrying someone not of noble birth had still been in place. She'd discovered they'd done the same thing to Tristan—paying off the parents of an English girl he'd loved and moving her to another part of the country. Tristan had been understandably bitter at their interference. Especially considering what a sham their parents' marriage was—the King still had a long-time mistress.

The history of unhappy, loveless marriages in

their family had made both her and Tristan deeply cynical about marriage. Fortunately Tristan had found Gemma. For Natalia there had been no one.

On a trip to Africa the previous year, to visit a girls' school that her charity had funded, she had travelled with an attractive photographer. Sparks had flown between them—not the kind of powerful attraction she'd felt instantly for Finn, but sparks just the same. But he had made it clear he would never get involved with her. Not when he knew his life would come under scrutiny and he would have to play second fiddle to a princess. Natalia had appreciated his honesty but had felt wounded because she hadn't even been given a chance.

That had been back then. Now Natalia wanted to shut the rest of the world out, so it shrank to just her and Finn. She resented the time spent chatting with the other six guests at their table. But politeness dictated that she distributed her time evenly. All that royal training in graciousness and good manners didn't go away just because she was in disguise.

The other guests were all pleasant people from Eliza's pre-Party Queens life. Natalia made it a point to chat with each of them. Finn joined in too, charming and thoughtful in his conversation. The others seemed to assume she and Finn were a couple, and neither of them did anything to make them think any differently.

One of the women was Chinese, and Finn surprised Natalia by exchanging a few words with her in her own language. 'You sound fluent in Chinese,' Natalia said when he turned his attention back to her.

'Thankfully, yes,' he said. 'One of my biggest new export markets is mainland China,' he explained. 'It's a great advantage to be able to speak Mandarin.'

'I can imagine,' she said.

'My grandfather spoke to me in Chinese when I was a child and my mother insisted I study the language formally when I was older. I studied Italian to please my grandmother—also useful for the business. And my sister Bella studied both languages too.'

Natalia wanted to tell him she was also multilingual, even chat to him in Italian, but it was too risky in case she tripped up over the details of a made-up background. The less she said about herself, the better. Pretending to be someone else, denying the truth about herself, wasn't as easy as she'd thought. Not when she really wanted to impress Finn.

'Sounds like your grandparents were very influential in your life,' she said.

Hers had been too. Her late paternal grandfa-

ther had been King when she was a child and had
ruled his family like a tyrant, although he'd been
seen as a benevolent ruler of the country. She'd
been terrified of him. Thankfully her mother
and father, despite their differences and the restrictions of their royal duties, had been united
in being loving parents to her and her brothers.

'My wonderful grandparents are both still
around, fortunately,' Finn said. 'I have them to
thank for my start in the business.'

Natalia hadn't mourned the death of her grandfather, and her grandmother had remained a dis-
tant, disapproving figure. She'd never known her
mother's parents.

'Really?' she said, fascinated to know every detail of his life in the short time she had with him.
Through him she could view life through a very
different lens. 'I'd love to hear about it.'

'My grandfather and grandmother met each
other in high school. It was like *Romeo and Juliet* set in the western suburbs of Sydney. His
family owned the local Chinese restaurant—her
family the Italian. Neither family was happy for
their child to marry out of their culture—the old
migrant story.'

Natalia leaned closer, sensing a real-life romance very different from her own family history of loveless arranged marriages. She was
better off being single than being pushed into

that kind of marriage—although to be fair to her parents, they had not pressured her, even when she'd said no to each of the unsuitable and unlovable six.

Anyway, how could you be sure of love? Her late brother Carl's marriage to Sylvie, the daughter of a duke, had supposedly been a 'love match'. Carl had been head over heels with her, and she'd seemed the same with him. But once she'd had her lavish wedding in the cathedral she'd proved to be greedy and avaricious, more in love with the wealth and status of being Crown Princess than with her husband. And there was no divorce for Montovian royalty. Make a bad choice and you were stuck with it for life.

'It must have been difficult for them if they had to defy their families,' she said.

'They say it only made them all the more determined to be together,' said Finn. 'Once they were twenty-one they could marry without their families' consent and they did. Fortunately they were both passionate about food, and my grandparents ended up running both restaurants. Their parents imported authentic ingredients from Asia and Europe, supplying other restaurants too. My *nonna* was a canny businesswoman and she soon grew the import side of the business so that it eclipsed the actual restaurants and they sold them.'

'So where did you come in?'

'I inherited their interest in food. However, my family also had a passion for education. I did a business degree at university, but worked all my vacations in the business. I went full-time when I graduated. I soon saw the opportunities for export as well as import. My grandparents handed the business over to me and I expanded it way beyond its original parameters. They still have a stake in it, but they're enjoying their retirement. I take all the risks.'

'Didn't your parents and your sister feel they'd been passed over?'

The rules for inheritance were very strict in Montovia—for everyone, not just royals.

'Not at all. My mother is a pharmacist. My father has his own construction company. My sister works with him. Seems we like keeping things in the family.'

'Sounds like your family is very close.'

'Yeah. It is. But that's enough about me. What about you?'

'My family story isn't as interesting as yours,' she said.

Of course it was—an unbroken line of rulers stretching back hundreds of years—but she couldn't share that.

'Just ordinary, really. I have a brother.' It was too painful to mention her other brother, whom she had adored; his loss still cut too deeply.

'My parents take rather too much interest in my life—which is annoying, considering I'm twenty-seven—but I guess that's okay.'

'It would be worse if they didn't take an interest, wouldn't it?' he said with a smile.

'True,' she said, returning his smile and gazing into his green eyes for rather longer than was polite on a shared table.

Their heads had been bowed closely together, their voices low for the duration of the conversation. Reluctantly she broke her gaze away and returned her attention to the other people at the table, as good manners dictated.

A pleasant middle-aged couple sat opposite them—Eliza's neighbours. Natalia and Finn chatted with them about how much they were enjoying the meal.

Once the plates for the main course had been cleared, the woman—Kerry—sat back in her chair. Her narrow-eyed gaze went from Natalia to Finn and back again. 'So, is all the romance of this lovely wedding giving you two ideas?' she said.

'I beg your pardon?' said Natalia, completely taken aback.

'You and Finn. Any plans for a wedding of your own?'

Natalia wasn't often lost for a diplomatic reply to an unexpected question. But the Australian woman's blunt questioning had her floundering. She looked up to Finn for help, only to see him struggling too.

'No plans yet,' he finally choked out.

'You haven't popped the question?'

'No!' he said.

'How long have you been together?'

'We…er…we only just met,' Natalia said, flushing hot with embarrassment.

The woman frowned. 'Really? Forgive me. It's just that…'

'Just that what?' Natalia prompted, suddenly curious.

'I've been around a while, and I can usually tell a perfectly matched couple. You two look so right together.'

Natalia gasped. She didn't dare look at Finn, and was at a complete loss as to what to say. But Finn diplomatically came to the rescue.

'I think we're right together too,' he said smoothly. 'But it's very early days.'

Natalia wished she could sink through the floor.

The woman smiled. 'I see a wedding and I'm never wrong,' she said, before turning her attention to her husband, who'd been trying to shush her.

Mortified, Natalia kept her eyes on her plate.

'Don't worry about her,' Finn murmured in her ear. 'She seems harmless. Unfortunately I seem to attract matchmakers. Weddings bring out the worst in them.'

If he only knew the level of matchmaking that had gone on—and continued to go on—when it came to Princess Natalia of Montovia. Finn O'Neill from Sydney, Australia—a merchant—would seem, in the eyes of her parents and the royal court, like a very unsuitable match indeed.

She was glad when the speeches started and she was able to turn away from the odd woman and any talk of matchmaking and marriage to face the top table.

CHAPTER THREE

THE SPEECHES WERE over and the bride and groom were dancing their first dance together. All the guests had been invited on to the dance floor to share the bridal waltz. At last Finn had Natalie in his arms—if only as a dance partner.

There was something intimate about an old-fashioned waltz. With her hand on his shoulder, his arms around her waist, she was kissing-distance close, her flowery perfume already familiar but no less alluring. Her body so near to his was warm, soft, sensual, and her innate rhythm kept them perfectly in step.

'You dance very well,' she said.

'I tried to get out of lessons at school but there was no escape.'

'You learned to waltz at *school*?'

'Private boys' school. Ballroom dancing was seen as a social skill. But I only waltz at weddings.' He twirled her around the room until she was breathless and laughing. 'You're a good dancer yourself.'

'I also had lessons,' she said.

Finn noticed she didn't elaborate in any of her answers. Perhaps her life really had been ordinary, even dull, although he wondered how someone as poised and vivacious as Natalie could come from dullness. Maybe she hadn't had the same opportunities in life he had been fortunate enough to have. Or the truth might be that her life hadn't been very happy and she was reticent about reliving an unhappy past even in social conversation.

Sometimes he was guilty of taking for granted the happy and supportive family life he enjoyed. This wedding—the happiness Eliza had found with Jake—had got him thinking. He wasn't as immune to wedding fever as he'd thought. Now, at the age of thirty-two, perhaps he did need to shake himself up, settle down and start a family of his own.

His *nonna* certainly thought that was the case. His broken engagement was ten years behind him—he could not in all reason continue to blame it for his aversion to marriage. He had to name it for what it was: an excuse—one he used to convince himself as well as others. The truth was that he hadn't met the right woman. Not one he could contemplate sharing his life with. When he did, he would willingly make that walk down the aisle. But he wouldn't compromise. And it wouldn't be any time soon—not when the business took up all his energy and time.

Perhaps...

He couldn't let himself think there was any

chance of Natalie being that woman. No matter what that crazy Kerry had said. No matter how he'd found himself agreeing with her that he and Natalie did feel right together. Not when Natalie was English. A tourist. Her home a twenty-two-hour plane ride away.

Long-distance dating had been a disaster with his former fiancée Chiara, the girl he'd met in Italy ten years back. Her level of treachery had left him bitter and broken.

The frequency of their phone calls had decreased. He'd been preoccupied with exams. But the day exams finished, on impulse he'd decided to make a surprise visit to Italy and booked a flight for the next day.

Chiara had been surprised, all right. Not only had she found herself another guy, she was pregnant. But she'd still hung on to Finn's engagement ring. He had vowed never, ever to try long-distance again. This—Natalie—was purely for the short term. He had to keep telling himself that.

'Those lessons paid off,' he said to Natalie now. 'You're very graceful.'

It felt as if they were dancing together in their own bubble of awareness. But the reality was that they were dancing alongside other guests. When would he be able to get her alone?

She looked up at him. 'That woman… Kerry. It was kind of weird, what she said.'

'Yes. But I wasn't lying when I agreed with her that something seems right about us being together.' He could hardly believe he was saying this to a woman he had only known for a matter of hours.

Her blue eyes widened. 'You meant that?'

'About the rightness? I feel it. Do you?'

Her forehead pleated in a frown. 'Yes. I… I think I do. But I don't understand—'

Finn felt a tap on his shoulder and turned to find a beaming Eliza and Jake cutting in on him and Natalie for their obligatory dances. He had no choice but to relinquish his intimate hold on the most gorgeous of women. He cursed under his breath that he hadn't got a chance to hear what Natalie had been about to say.

Reluctantly he let her go and watched Natalie waltz away with Jake, smiling up at him. A spasm of jealousy shuddered through him at the sight of his beautiful dance partner in the arms of another man—even though Jake was a newly-wed husband who adored his new wife.

What was happening here?

He'd only just met Natalie. He hardly knew her. But he'd never felt such a connection with a woman—if that was what you called something so compelling. He'd dated. He'd had steady girlfriends. He'd been engaged. But none of those relationships had started with a lightning bolt from nowhere.

'Surely you can take your eyes off her for long enough to speak to me?' said Eliza drily as he danced with his friend the bride.

'What do you mean?' he blustered.

'You're mesmerised by Natalie. She's beautiful. Charming. I get it. But you need to back off from her, Finn. She's not for you.'

'This is about Prue, isn't it?' He gritted his teeth. 'How many times do I have to tell you I'm not interested?'

'Even so, it was rude of you to change those place cards. What on earth got into you to do such a thing?'

Eliza had always been an outspoken kind of friend.

He shrugged. 'Sorry.'

But he wasn't sorry at all, and Eliza's sigh told him she knew it.

'This can't end well. That's all I can say.'

In spite of himself, he felt a chill of foreboding. 'Are you telling me that Natalie has a criminal record or—?'

Eliza looked aghast. 'Of course not. Don't be ridiculous.'

'Is she after my money?' he joked.

Ever since that Sunday newspaper had included

him in a list of the most eligible young million-aires he'd been plagued by women whose interest in him was purely mercenary. Which had made him even more cynical about relationships.

'I very much doubt it,' Eliza said. 'She's just not for you. You'll have to trust me on this.'

He snorted his disbelief. 'You're warning me off? In the meantime, your neighbour Kerry is suggesting I propose to Natalie because we seem so perfect together.'

'What?'

'Yeah. In fact she asked if we'd made wedding plans.'

'Really?' Eliza frowned. 'Kerry reckons she's psychic. She… Well, she wouldn't say that if she didn't believe it was true.'

Finn rolled his eyes. 'Psychic? *Huh!* She seemed nice enough until she came out with *that* nonsense.'

'What's stranger still is that her predictions often come true. The first time she met Jake she told me I'd marry him. It seemed highly unlikely at the time.'

'Coincidence—a lucky guess,' Finn said dismissively.

'Superstitious nonsense?' Eliza said.

Finn agreed. The trouble was, he came from three cultures where superstitions were taken seriously. By the older generation, that was. Not by him. He was a facts and numbers man.

'But it was disconcerting,' he admitted.

'In this case she's got it wrong,' Eliza said. 'I'll say it again—back off from Natalie.'

'You're seriously warning me, Eliza?'

'As a friend. Yes.'

'And as a friend, I appreciate your concern—although I don't know where it's coming from. But I'd rather you wished me luck than tossed a bucket of cold water over me. Because I like Natalie and I'm going to continue to enjoy her company for the rest of the evening.' He kissed her on the cheek. 'Thank you for the dance. Again, congratulations to you and Jake. Now I'm going to march over there to your husband and claim my dance partner back.'

Natalia couldn't remember when she'd so enjoyed a man's company. Dancing with Finn, their steps perfectly matched, was magic. Chatting with him, laughing with him, deepened the spell.

But the enchanted evening was winding down. The bride and groom had left to a chorus of good wishes for their honeymoon and a long life together. Other guests were starting to disperse and the band had announced the last number for the evening.

Soon the big room would echo with empti-

ness. Her bodyguards would be discreetly waiting to escort her back to the harbour-side hotel
where she was booked in under her Natalie Gerard name. She would never see Finn again. She
felt plunged into gloom at the thought.

The last dance was a slow one and they danced
it close together. She breathed in the scent of him,
felt his warm breath ruffling her hair. All sorts
of potential conversations were running through
her head. But all she managed was to look up at
him and stutter. 'I… I don't want the night to end.'

His green eyes met hers. 'Neither do I.'

Too many hopes and possibilities were trembling on her lips for her actually to articulate the
words *I want to be with you.* But finally she managed to choke out an invitation of sorts—although
not the one she really wanted to communicate.

'I'm staying at a lovely hotel. It has a very smart
bar, open all hours. Would you like to come back
for a drink? Or a coffee? Or…?' Her voice trailed
away. She was articulate in five languages, yet
she was stumbling on a simple offer to extend the
evening with a drink in a bar.

He tilted her chin, so his gaze met hers. 'Yes—
to whatever you're offering.'

'I have a car and driver booked,' she said. And
there would be another car with the second bodyguard following.

'Cancel it. Let me drive you in my car,' he said.

For a moment she was tempted. There was nothing she would have liked better than to be alone with Finn in his car. But 'living dangerously' had its limitations. The helicopter accident that had claimed the lives of her brother, his wife and their toddler son had been an accident, not an assassination. But after such a tragedy, security for the remaining heirs had become an obsession with the royal family. She could not dismiss her bodyguards.

'I can't do that, I'm afraid,' she said. She held her breath. Would that be a deal-breaker for Finn? 'You would have to come in my car. Or we could go to the hotel separately and meet there.'

'I'll ride with you.' Did he, like her, not want to waste a moment of the limited time they had together?

She sighed her relief. 'Good. My driver is outside. I'll call him and tell him we'll have an extra passenger.'

Would Finn wonder why she should do that? Most hire car drivers wouldn't have to be notified of an extra passenger.

'I'll have to go back to the table and retrieve my handbag. My phone's in it,' she said.

'As long as you come straight back to me,' he said, in that deep husky voice.

'Count on it,' she said, thrilled by the look in his eyes.

She called her bodyguards and provided Finn's name. She knew they would immediately run a security check on him. Perhaps she was being foolish, but she felt sure nothing untoward would come up on the check. She scarcely knew him, but she felt she could trust him to be who he said he was. It was she who was twisting the truth about herself right out of shape.

'Ready to go?' Finn said when she returned to his side.

'The car will come around to the front to pick us up,' she said.

He put a possessive arm around her as they headed outside. She leaned into him, loving the closeness to his strength and warmth. Then felt bereft when she moved away from him for the sake of appearances as they reached the main doors.

The street level entrance to the grand old house was bracketed by tall palm trees and large old-fashioned carriage lamps. Cars and taxis inched forward on the circular driveway to pick up the departing wedding guests. Natalia spotted the unobtrusive dark sedan driven by her bodyguard in the line-up. The other bodyguard wouldn't be far away. Their orders were to be close by always.

She could not fault her parents for taking such good care of her, even if it did seem irksome at times. The terrible loss of her brother and his family—not just Carl, but precious two-year-old

Rudolph, whom they'd all adored, and his mother Sylvie—had thrown them into despair.

Tristan had been forced to step up into a role he'd felt ill-prepared for. Natalia had been thrust into being second in line to the throne and her freedom had been severely curtailed.

Becoming second in line to a throne after a sudden death was a different matter altogether from being fourth in line behind three male heirs. She'd gone from being relatively independent to being cosseted. And the campaign to get her married to someone suitable and bearing further heirs had been stepped up. She'd begun to feel trapped—albeit in a golden cage—stifled, and more than a touch rebellious. She'd been determined to get permission to leave Montevia and attend this wedding.

Much as she railed against the stepped-up security, she could see the reasons why. But nothing was going to stop her enjoying every minute available to her with Finn.

She followed him to take their places near the cluster of guests waiting for their cars. Thankfully, Tristan and Gemma were not among them to see her looking so cosy with Finn. Her brother and his wife had left early because Gemma hadn't been feeling well. On the dance floor, Natalia had done nothing to earn her brother's disapproval.

That might not be the case by the time the evening was through.

It soon became obvious that they were going to have to wait a few minutes for her car. She didn't want to wait a second longer to be alone with Finn.

He seemed to feel the same. 'We don't have to get caught up in banal conversation about why the traffic is backed up,' he said. 'C'mon.'

Just a few steps took them away from the other guests until they stood shoulder to shoulder by the side of the portico, away from the lamps that lit the entrance, private in the shadow of a large camellia tree studded with luminous white blooms. Huge tubs of exotic flowering orchids hid them from general view—plants she would only see in a greenhouse back home. The air was rich with the scent of jasmine, romantic and intoxicating.

Everything about Australia was so different from her homeland of snow-capped mountains, vast lakes and the sharp scent of pine needles. And Finn was so different from any man she had ever met. Different in such an exciting way.

So far away from home she wasn't bound by the rules.

She shivered—not just because of a gust of cool, early spring air but because she felt a sudden nervousness about finally being alone with him and what she hoped that might lead to.

He turned to face her. 'Are you cold?'

'Just the breeze,' she said, wrapping her arms around herself, not wanting to betray how she was feeling about him.

Finn stepped closer, his gaze intent on her face. In the poorly lit gloom his eyes gleamed green. She forgot to shiver, almost forgot to breathe, seeing the expression in his eyes, the sensual set of his mouth. Her heart started thudding so erratically that surely he could hear it.

He gently disengaged her arms and held her hands by her side, his hands warm on her bare skin. For a long moment he looked into her eyes, and questions and answers were silently exchanged. Her lips parted in anticipation as he lowered his mouth to hers and she sighed with pleasure as he kissed her.

At last.

His mouth was warm and firm on hers in a kiss that was sure and demanding while gentle at the same time. Her eyes closed as she savoured the closeness of him and she kissed him back.

She was just getting into the rhythm of kisses given and returned when he broke the contact. She swallowed a whimper of dismay at the loss—she didn't want to sound needy.

'I've wanted to kiss you for hours,' he said, in that so-sexy deep voice.

'Me too,' she said. 'Kiss *you*, I mean. Please… please don't stop.'

He laughed, low and triumphant, and then kissed her again. His touch ignited the hunger for him that had been brewing since the moment she'd seen him. She'd been without a man in her life for a long time, but this wasn't just hunger for a man's touch—it was hunger for *him*, this man, Finn.

His tongue slid between her lips to meet hers. He let go of her hands to put his arms around her and draw her closer. She wound her arms around his neck and returned his kiss, loving the feel of his tongue, his lips, the taste of him. Starbursts of sensation seemed to ignite along every pleasure pathway.

He certainly knew how to kiss. And the fact that he was experienced was a point in his favour. She wanted a man who knew what he was doing.

Yes. Finn was the one. There was no doubt in her mind.

Tonight, she wanted to lose her virginity to Finn.

CHAPTER FOUR

NATALIA COULD NOT get enough of Finn's kisses. *She could not get enough of Finn.* But did her kisses, so enthusiastically returned, betray her lack of experience? Could he guess at her untouched state?

The thoughts plagued her as the sound of her name being called—her fake name—made her reluctantly break away from his kiss to see that her car had reached the head of the line.

She had to take a moment to compose herself, and noticed with a secret thrill that Finn had to do the same. Then, with a gentlemanly hand on her elbow, he steered her to where the driver, cap firmly down to shield his face, held the door open for her.

She hoped the remaining guests waiting for their transport were too busy chatting among themselves to notice the signs of recent passionate kisses on an incognito princess slinking out from the shadows—her flushed face, her lack of lipstick, her tousled hair... Then she realised that because she was incognito no one would care. She was just another guest at a wedding.

The anonymity thrilled her.

Of course she'd been kissed before. Mostly

by frogs, but also by a few genuine princes. But she'd never gone much further than kissing. Duty again. It was expected that a royal Montovian bride would be a virgin. Her marriage would be more about alliances and political strategy than passionate love. There had to be no doubt that any children born to the union were her husband's legitimate offspring.

The necessity for her to stay chaste until marriage had been drummed into her from the time she'd understood what it was all about. But she hadn't expected to still be a virgin at age twenty-seven. It was a situation she was beginning to find onerous. Most of her friends were married—mothers, even—while she was still wondering what it was like to make love with a man.

In the hours since she'd met Finn, she'd found herself even more curious.

She'd been expected to marry young to a suitable man of noble birth chosen for her by her parents. Her refusal to marry any of the palace-approved contenders had meant she had stayed single—and celibate—for far longer than might have been expected. She'd also had a full year in mourning for her brother, and had been uninterested in dating during those dark days.

In retrospect, it was fortunate that she hadn't allowed herself to be talked into marrying any of those 'suitable' men who'd proposed. Tristan had recently had the rules changed to allow Montovian royals to marry commoners, so he could marry Gemma, an Australian chef. The new rule hadn't really been tested, though, as Gemma had discovered a connection to British royalty. But Natalia was now, in theory, allowed to marry who she wanted.

However, the King and Queen were resisting that idea when it came to their daughter. The ace they held in their hand was that she had to get their permission to marry, whether the man was royal or not. So had Carl. As had Tristan. And Natalia knew they had a nerdy twenty-two-year-old duke lined up for her to meet when she got home. She'd promised to be nice to him, as the only other aristocrat on offer was his widowed uncle the Grand Duke, who'd just had a double hip replacement.

Now, she squirmed in her seat with the effort of keeping a discreet distance from Finn in the back seat of the car. She wanted more kisses. More caresses. *More Finn.* Her nipples tightened at the thought of it. And when he reached across the seat to take her hand in his she nearly jumped through the roof of the car at the sensual thrill that simple touch ignited.

There was another reason she was still a virgin at twenty-seven. She hadn't met anyone who had tempted her. If she had, she might have defied duty and lost her virginity before. But no man had aroused her desire.

Until now.

Finn prided himself on his ability to stay in control under any circumstance. He didn't permit himself to be distracted by emotion. His cool level-headedness in negotiation was one of the reasons he was so successful in business. Plus, he had an instinct to know when to take a strategic risk—perhaps honed by all those childhood games of mah-jong with his grandfather.

But the feelings that surged through him now, just holding hands with Natalie, had him stymied. He wanted her so badly he ached. As a rule, he was cautious about trusting strangers. He'd learned that in both his business and personal life. But in Natalie's case caution simply didn't come into it. He didn't know her, and yet he felt he knew all he needed to know.

However Eliza wouldn't have warned him off her without reason. Every instinct shouted that Natalie might not be telling him everything about herself. But he didn't care.

He just wanted her.

In the back seat of the limo it was all he could do to stay a respectable distance from her. Her fingers entwined with his was their only contact. Her dress had ridden up over her knees, despite her efforts to keep it modestly tugged down, treating him to an enticing glimpse of bare, slender thighs. When the driver took a corner sharply she slid closer, so her thigh nudged his. He had to invoke every ounce of restraint not to reach out and put his hand on her bare skin, push the skirt higher.

Lustful thoughts fogged his brain, but another insistent thought wound its way through the want and the need. *This woman was special*. It wasn't just about sex. She fascinated him. He hadn't believed the so-called psychic when she'd predicted a future for him and Natalie. Yet one crazy, unrestrained part of him wanted to.

It was all he could do not to pull her into his arms and take advantage of the privacy the back seat allowed. But he'd noticed Natalie's quick, nervous glances at their driver. The back seat was not private enough for her and he respected that. This had happened unexpectedly. He would let her lead the way. Whatever she was willing to give, he was willing to take.

He was surprised when the car pulled up in front of a five-star hotel in one of the best locations in the city—right on the edge of the harbour, situated between the icons of the Sydney Harbour Bridge and the Opera House. Somehow he had expected more modest accommodation—

but then this limousine was hardly a budget ride ordered from an app.

It seemed the world of fashion was treating Natalie well. Which, to his relief, put paid to any lingering thought that she might be interested in what he had rather than who he was. As far as he knew, they were total strangers who had met by chance at a wedding. How could she know the extent of his wealth?

She thanked the driver graciously as the man held the door open for her. Then turned to wait for Finn to follow her out of the car. He nodded his thanks to the driver, but in truth he hardly noticed the guy. And he scarcely took in the elegant hotel entrance, the glass walls that looked directly through to the water, the uniformed doormen...

Natalie. She was the only sight that interested him and he could not keep his eyes off her.

She was flushed high on her cheekbones and her mouth, swollen from his kisses, was parted in an enigmatic half-smile. Her gaze was as focused on him as his was on her. Her eyes were the most extraordinary shade of iris-blue—he had only seen eyes like them before on one other person, although he couldn't for the life of him remember who it was.

Not that it mattered. Natalie's eyes were the only eyes that interested him. Ditto Natalie's face. Natalie's body. Natalie's soul. He wanted to discover more about her, to know what made her tick, nail down what it was about her that he found so extraordinarily appealing. He was tense, coiled— impatient to be alone with her. And not just for this evening. For the remainder of her stay in Sydney.

He could not let himself think beyond that, much as his thoughts strained to go there.

Gritting his teeth against his impatience, he followed her through the foyer of the hotel, all marble and glass and luxury appointments. 'So, what's it to be?' he asked, forcing himself to sound laid-back. 'The bar? Coffee?'

Her flush deepened and she looked down before she looked up. Natalie was a hot, sexy woman, and he suspected she would give as good as she got in bed. Yet there was a reticence in her that made her even more appealing.

He would enjoy peeling back the layers of her personality as much as he would enjoy peeling that pink dress from her body. It closed with a long zipper at the back—he'd done a recce on it when she had been kissing him so sensationally behind those pots of orchids.

'I thought, perhaps, my room,' she said. 'We could order room service. Whatever you want.'

He pulled her close enough to whisper in her ear. 'I don't want coffee. I only want you. Your room sounds like a great idea.'

Finn felt a shiver go through her. It wasn't the

cold this time. With a rising sense of elation he realised her shiver was one of anticipation.

He was exalted by a feeling that had nothing to do with reason, rationality, common sense. Tonight might be the start of something that switched him to a different track. Despite the odds—and her living in another country—Natalie could become someone so much more than a time-stamped encounter at a wedding.

'Let's go, then,' she murmured as she slipped her hand into his.

They had the elevator to themselves. He only let her go long enough for her to tap the key card for her room number before he pulled her to him in a hungry, urgent kiss. With a murmur of need and pleasure that made his heart thud she kissed him back with equal urgency, looping her arms around his neck and drawing him closer.

Three walls and the ceiling of the elevator were mirrored, and he could see her reflection in all of them—sexy, vibrant Natalie, in her clinging pink dress, all curves and blonde hair tumbling untamed down her back.

He felt his life had been lived in black and white until she had flashed into it in a glorious kaleidoscope of glittering blue eyes and shiny red lips and the flash of diamonds from her earrings. He was enveloped by her as she pressed her curves against him, as he breathed in her heady scent—

all his senses were invaded and overwhelmed by the urgency of his need for her.

When the elevator doors glided open they were both momentarily stunned by the interruption. She broke the kiss, looked up at him from the circle of his arms, and started to laugh—a delightful sound that prompted a smile from him in response. He didn't let her go, rather walked her out of the elevator, mumbled a question about the direction of her room, and then kissed her again.

He joined in her laughter as they kissed and stumbled their way up the corridor. Alternating laughter with kisses, they staggered to her room—a spacious suite with glass doors to a balcony framing a view of the harbour and the night-lit Opera House. An enormous bed dominated the room.

They were finally alone, and their laughter faded, vanquished by kisses of increasing intensity, their breath coming in gasps and sighs.

'I… I haven't done this before,' Natalia murmured, somewhere between him caressing her through her dress and locating the pull of her zipper.

Hadn't taken a man back to her hotel room on such short acquaintance? Something about the edge of nervousness to her voice led him to believe her.

'You don't have to do anything you don't want to,' he said.

'Er... I—I haven't lived this dangerously, I mean,' she said, stuttering a little.

'Let me help you enjoy life on the edge,' he said, tugging on her zipper.

'You're still my tutor?'

'Always,' he said.

He pulled down the zipper, the sound of it echoing in the empty room, and started to push her dress off her shoulders, making each movement a caress. He kissed along the delicate hollows of her throat, across her shoulders, down towards the swell of her breasts.

She gasped with surprised pleasure. Then shrugged her shoulders to help him free her of her dress. It slid to the floor, where it pooled around her feet before she stepped out of it, leaving her in a lacy pink bra and panties. He drew in a breath of admiration and excitement. Her body was perfection—creamy skin, curves in the right places, long slender legs.

She went to kick off her stilettoes. 'Leave them,' he said, scarcely able to choke out the words. He had never seen a sexier, more beautiful sight than Natalie clad in just her underwear and her high-heeled shoes.

For Natalia, being stripped down to her underwear in front of a man was something new, but she found she wasn't nervous. Instinctively, she trusted Finn to guide her through this momentous journey. Besides, she was too caught up in the moment to worry about what might come next. Kissing Finn, she was overwhelmed by sensation, by the promise of his hard, muscular body intimately close to hers, the pleasure his clever hands and mouth were giving her.

Even his most fleeting touch ignited starbursts of sensation, made her throb in places she hadn't known could throb. She wanted more. So much more. *Finn.*

'We need to even the score here,' she murmured, impatient with the feel of his jacket against her exposed skin. She ached for skin on skin.

With hands that weren't quite steady she pushed aside his jacket. He took over, sliding his arms out of the sleeves, tossing the jacket without aim so that it fell discarded on the carpet. She went to unfasten his dress shirt and found not buttons but fiddly studs that presented a momentary setback. She fumbled through with a semblance of confidence—she didn't want him to guess this was the first time she'd undressed a man—then got the bow tie unfurled and discarded.

Silently Finn held up his hands and she saw that his sleeves fastened with cufflinks in the shape of tiny compasses—white gold with black stones she realised were black diamonds. No tossing *those* on the floor. She hastily placed them and the bow tie on the narrow table set along the wall, impatient to strip him of his shirt.

As she pushed his shirt off his shoulders and to the floor Natalia gasped. She had to quickly disguise her sudden intake of breath as a cough. Finn bare-chested was even more impressive than Finn fully clothed. Broad shoulders, sculpted arms, chest firmly defined, his belly flat and taut, with just a dusting of dark body hair. His olive skin was smooth and warm beneath her touch.

She took a step back to feast her eyes on him. 'You are the most beautiful man,' she murmured, scarcely able to get the words out with the quickening of her breath. She felt almost faint with desire.

'Beautiful?' he said, with a quirk of his dark brows. 'That's a word I'd apply to you, the most beautiful woman at the wedding. Now I have you all to myself.'

'A man can be beautiful, can't he? But I'll say handsome if you prefer. Though even handsome isn't enough to describe your...your perfection.'

'I'm blushing,' he said.

But he wasn't. He was smiling. And his eyes narrowed further with a look of intensity that let her know she was about to be kissed again. Eager for his touch, she parted her lips to welcome him, pressed herself closer to him, her softness against his strength.

When he cupped her breast in his hand she almost screamed with the pleasure of it. In turn, she explored him, his skin smooth and warm over hard muscles, his reaction letting her know he enjoyed what she was doing. She kissed a trail down his throat and he moaned his appreciation. His reaction excited her, taking her to heights she hadn't known existed.

There wasn't much clothing left between them, and as she felt Finn grasp the fastening of her bra she realised there soon wouldn't be even that. She plucked up the courage to find the fastening of his belt, with the aim of undoing it, but it wasn't as straightforward as she'd thought. It was impossible to concentrate on anything other than the sensations Finn was arousing in her.

Her legs were beginning to buckle beneath her from the intensity of her pleasure, the ache of anticipation. That big bed was beckoning.

She broke away from the kiss. Finn followed the direction of her gaze. 'Yes,' he said.

Effortlessly, he swept her up in his arms.

'You…you're going to carry me to the bed?'

She'd thought this kind of thing only happened in movies. The thrill was immeasurable. She couldn't wait to be initiated by Finn into the mysteries of making love.

'That's my intention,' he said. He paused. 'But first, protection.'

Protection? For a moment she didn't realise what he meant. Protection in case he dropped her? Then it dawned on her. She hadn't ever been in need of the kind of protection he meant.

She couldn't meet his gaze, rather looked out over his shoulder at the view of Sydney Harbour. 'I…er… I'm not protected.'

He groaned. 'I wasn't expecting… I don't have anything.'

'Then we can't—?'

'No. But no doubt the hotel stocks—'

'You…you mean order them from room service?' she said faintly.

'Or visit the concierge,' he said.

Natalia stilled in his arms as the full impact of what they were discussing hit her. *She couldn't do this.* What had seemed romantic, rebellious and rather racy suddenly seemed very, very foolish. There would be consequences if she flaunted the rules. Protection was called protection for a reason. Protection against pregnancy being one of them.

She was a royal princess. What if she got pregnant from a vacation fling—for that was all it could be with Finn. What if she were recognised? What if someone saw Finn go down to the concierge to buy protection and then go up to her room?

She wanted Finn. Wanted him so badly that

for a moment there she'd almost been prepared to take the risk of saying yes to no protection. *But she couldn't have him.* Not like this.

Duty. Honour. Responsibility. *Doing the right thing.* They were values ingrained in her very being. How could she ever have thought she could evade them? She was the Princess of Montovia and as such she did not have flings. She might be pretending to be just an ordinary girl but she wasn't.

The rules and restrictions were there for a reason—and she had to live by them. Not play risky games. It might seem terribly old-fashioned, but that was the way it was in Montovia. She and Tristan and Gemma were working together to stretch the boundaries when it came to contemporary life—but they weren't there yet.

A sob rose up in her throat and she swallowed it. To make love with Finn was too much of a risk for her to take—no matter how much she wanted him. No matter how much she liked him. This wasn't the way to lose her virginity.

She remembered the security guards in the adjoining room. They would be aware she had invited a stranger to her room. They might very well be listening via some device to ensure she was safe. Nausea struck her at the thought of them hearing what she and Finn had been murmuring to each other. But even if they were not, a full report of her behaviour would go back to the King and Queen.

What if she didn't care? What if she decided to make love with Finn completely on her own terms? *And then never saw him again?* The answer—emotional agony. She wanted to lose her virginity with a man who would be part of her life for more than one night.

Finn still held her aloft in his arms. But she couldn't stay there. Not now.

She wiggled to be let down. Finn immediately released her and held her until she was steady on her feet.

'You okay?' he asked with a puzzled frown.

How could she have this kind of conversation while standing in only her bra and panties and a pair of high heels?

She took a deep breath in an effort to steady her racing pulse. 'Not really. No. I...er... About the protection... I... I...don't think we'll need it. We need to stop. You see, I—'

'This is moving too quickly for you?' His voice was gruff, but not unkind.

She nearly collapsed with gratitude at his understanding. For just plain Natalie, it had been going just fine. She ached for more, to discover what making love to Finn would be like—utterly, mind-blowingly wonderful, she suspected. But for

Princess Natalia, this had gone too far already. She had stepped right out of bounds.

Mutely, she nodded. 'Er...yes,' she finally managed to choke out, wary of his reaction and unable to look at him, focusing on the toes of her stilettos instead.

She'd heard what men called women who led men on and then said no and it wasn't pleasant. She was still throbbing with desire for him, and he must feel at least as frustrated as she was.

'It's not that I'm not enjoying this—I am, very much—but—'

He reached out to her, placed his fingers under her chin and tilted her face up so she was forced to look at him. 'It's too soon. I get that. I want you, but only if you're ready.'

No calling her a tease. No frustrated anger.

'I... I...' How could she explain when to do so would mean having to untangle the web of lies she'd woven since the moment she'd met him? 'As I said earlier, I haven't done this before.'

She hadn't done *any* of this before. She could only imagine how surprised he would be if she admitted to her virginity.

Finn stood there, unbearably handsome in just his trousers, the belt looped where she had attempted to tug it loose.

'No need to explain,' he said. 'You're worth the wait, Natalie.'

'Th…thank you. But you…you should probably go,' she said.

'If that's what you want,' he said.

He looked around for his clothes, so joyously removed by her in anticipation of what she now would never experience with him.

Mutely, she nodded. Suddenly self-conscious, she reached for the luxurious velour robe provided by the hotel and shrugged into it. She went to wrap it around her waist.

Finn watched her, his eyes half hooded in sensual awareness. 'No need to do that robe up. I like the view with it open so much better.'

'Oh…' she said, blushing. 'I'm glad. That… that you like the view, I mean.'

She took a step towards him. He took a step back.

'Don't tempt me, Natalie. I might not be as strong-minded if I have you too close.'

'Of course,' she said.

She really didn't know how to behave. This was all new territory for her.

'Have you been sailing on the harbour?' he asked as he put on his shirt.

She was taken aback by the sudden change of subject. Then she realised the effort it was taking for him to turn the conversation to something other than their thwarted sexual escapade.

'I've ridden the ferries,' she said. 'I took the Manly ferry all the way to Manly.'

He laughed. 'Not quite the same. How about I swing around here tomorrow and pick you up? I'll take you out on my yacht—we can have lunch on the water.'

'You have a yacht?' she asked, stalling.

She couldn't in all honesty accept his invitation. Yet to outright decline it would entwine her in a more knotted tangle of lies. She realised she was twisting her hands together, something she did when agitated, and forced herself to stop it.

'A very beautiful yacht.'

He shrugged on his jacket, swept up his bow tie and cufflinks and shoved them carelessly into his pocket. Such a shame to cover that expanse of splendid male body, she thought with fleeting sadness.

'The best place to see Sydney is from the water. You'd love it.'

She couldn't call herself a sailor, but there was nothing she would like more than to be on a boat with Finn. If it were in any way possible she would jump at the chance.

'I'm sure I would,' she murmured.

'I'll see you at ten tomorrow morning,' he said. 'I'll call to confirm.'

'That would be nice,' she said.

It *would* be nice. But she would not be here at ten o'clock tomorrow morning.

She looked up at him. At his open shirt collar, his thick straight black hair dishevelled by her caresses, his handsome, handsome face, his intelligent, kind eyes…

'Finn, I'm sorry about tonight. How things ended. Or…or didn't end. I—'

'No apologies. No explanations. It moved too fast for you. We have tomorrow.'

'Er…yes.'

Tomorrow would come, but not for them.

He took her in his arms, kissed her swift and hard on the mouth. 'I wasn't keen on going to the wedding—I expected it to be insufferably boring. But it turned out to be anything but boring. Because of you.'

'The wedding was…magical. Because of *you*.'

She reached up to trace her fingers down his cheek to the corner of his mouth, frantic to store his face in her memory.

He caught her hand and kissed the centre of her palm. It was almost unbearably pleasurable.

'Tomorrow can be magical too. There's something very special about being out on the harbour. You'll see.'

'Yes…' she said, the word trailing away.

'I have to go, or I might be tempted to talk you

out of your decision. Goodnight, Natalie,' he said, and turned towards the door.

'Wait.' She reached up, cradled his face in her hands. 'Thank you, Finn. Thank you for your patience with me. Thank you for…for everything. The best thing I ever did was switch those place cards. I had the most wonderful time with you. More wonderful than you can imagine.'

She kissed him on his mouth, slow and lingering, for the last time.

'I… I don't know how to say goodbye,' she said, choking up.

'Then don't,' he said. *'Alla prossima,* as we say in Italian.'

'Until we meet again,' she translated.

'You speak Italian?' he said.

She nodded.

'There's so much I don't know about you,' he said slowly.

If only he knew just how much.

She would cry if he stayed any longer. Sob and beg him to stay, spill the truth about her deception, beg him to forgive her for her lies.

But she had sworn to her family to tell no one in Australia the truth of her identity. And the habits of duty and obedience were impossible to break. Especially with the fragile state her parents had been in since Carl's death.

'And me about you,' she murmured.

'We'll have to remedy that,' he said, looking down into her face, a slight frown creasing his brow as if he guessed that all might not be as it seemed.

She put up her hand in farewell. *'Ciao, bello,'* she murmured. *Farewell, beautiful man.*

'Ciao, bella,' he said. 'The most beautiful girl at the wedding.'

She smiled shakily. 'I don't know that the groom would agree.'

'It's what *I* think that counts,' he said. 'See you in the morning.'

He turned, opened the door and walked away, turning back once for a final smile.

Natalie watched him go until he disappeared around the corner of the corridor. Then she let the door slam loudly behind him in frustration and anger at herself—and to make it clear to her security guards that her visitor was not staying. Scandal averted.

Immediately she regretted letting him go. Realised she might have made the biggest mistake of her life.

She would never see Finn again.

When he got here tomorrow morning he would be informed at the desk that Ms Gerard had checked out. What the hotel wouldn't know— what Finn would never know—was that Princess Natalia of Montovia, along with her brother the

Crown Prince and his wife the Crown Princess, had flown out of Sydney early in the morning on the royal family's private jet and headed home to their ancestral palace.

She dragged one foot in front of the other back into the room, now achingly empty of Finn's presence—but stopped when she noticed something glinting on the carpet. A cufflink. One white gold cufflink in the shape of a compass, its face picked out in tiny black diamonds. It must have slipped from his pocket.

She picked it up. Was it fanciful to think that it still felt warm from his body?

She held it to her heart and let the tears of regret and lost opportunity flow.

CHAPTER FIVE

Three months later. Royal palace of Montovia.

NATALIA DRESSED FOR dinner with her family almost automatically. She had her own private apartment within the palace, as did Tristan and Gemma. But she was expected to attend the regular receptions, rich with the trappings of royalty, in the state dining area, where the King and Queen entertained dignitaries both from Montovia and other countries.

Increasingly, Tristan, in his role as Crown Prince, invited people of strategic importance to their country, and also to the business interests he oversaw. Natalia hadn't requested an invitation for anyone since she'd got back from Australia. It seemed too much effort.

She slipped into a full-length gown in midnight-blue silk, embellished with embroidery and crystals, beautiful in its simplicity and perfect cut. She teamed it with elegant stilettos covered in silk dyed the same shade of blue and scattered with crystals. She fastened earrings glittering with sapphires and diamonds and a matching bracelet. But she took little joy in her outfit.

Since her return from Australia she'd had to

invest in a new wardrobe as she'd dropped two dress sizes. To someone with her interest in fashion, and the almost unlimited budget of a princess, shopping should have been a delight. Not so.

She was too down in the dumps to appreciate how lucky she was to be replenishing her wardrobe in the fashion capitals of Paris, Milan and London. Too unmotivated to appreciate what a boost her now too-large wardrobe would give to her next auction. Too darn exhausted to put 100 per cent into working alongside Tristan in promoting Montovia's export business—something she'd wanted to do for ages. Too heartsore to engage in anything much but endless agonising about 'what might have been' with Finn.

To her friends who asked about her weight loss secret, what diet she'd followed to get so skinny so fast, she had no reply. Not an honest one anyway. She had sworn to keep her incognito visit to Sydney a secret. That meant she couldn't confide in anyone the exhilaration of being Natalie Gerard, or the consequent deep dip in her spirits since she'd returned home.

Gemma knew about the trip, of course, but she couldn't talk to her either, because that would mean confiding in her sister-in-law the emotional rollercoaster of her time with Finn. The high of her powerful attraction to him, the shared laughter and the fun. The soaring excitement of his kisses and caresses. The plunge into misery as she'd watched Finn walk away.

No, the regret, self-recrimination and guilt were all hers to suffer on her own, often in the restless, sleepless hours after midnight. She had not wanted to lose weight, but her 'diet secret' could be put down to loss of appetite, trouble sleeping and the thoughts of Finn that plagued her like a repeat cycle she couldn't switch off, making her feel on the edge of anxiety.

She had run away from the only man she had ever wanted. Over and over she had relived that scene in her hotel bedroom. Wondered again and again what it would have been like if she had let Finn carry her to that bed. Regretted more times than she could count that she hadn't gone all the way with him. Only to realise that if she had, how much worse leaving him would have been.

Or what if she hadn't left? Why hadn't she even entertained a plan of simply informing Tristan she would not be flying back in the royal jet but rather staying to enjoy a day's sailing on the harbour before going home on a commercial flight when she was ready.

Because she would have had to tell the truth about her identity.

She sighed as she gave a final smoothing to the back of her hair. Her day-to-day life was fulfilling, what with her charity duties and her work with Tristan. Although somehow, caught up in her grief over Carl and her parents' obsession with the line of succession, she had gone backwards in terms of personal freedom as she got older rather than moving forward. But that was her life right now, and she wasn't sure what she could do to break out of it.

Other than run away to Sydney and find Finn...

Now, she headed down in the elevator to the state rooms, weary at the thought of having to divide her time equally between the person on her right and the one on her left, making polite, diplomatic small talk that would advance the interests of her country.

When had the thrill gone out of such occasions? Had they ever been more than endless duty and obligation?

Mentally she chastised herself for such ungrateful thoughts—she led a life of unimaginable privilege and should be unquestioningly thankful that she had won the lottery of noble birth. But a nagging thought kept intruding—the happiest days of her life had been those when she'd roamed incognito around Sydney, her only real obligation being to hide her identity. The happiest hours of all were when she'd been with Finn.

It always came back to Finn.

Natalia pasted on her most regal smile. As both Princess and dutiful daughter, her role was to be gracious and charming to the guests while cocktails and canapés were served before a formal dinner. She chatted to both people she knew and people she didn't, switching from one language to another as required. She felt her parents' approving glances upon her. This was what she'd been trained for, but since her time in laidback Australia she sometimes felt like an outsider, looking in on the rituals that she had been part of since birth.

Her smile was beginning to feel forced by the time she caught sight of Tristan walking into the room, deep in conversation with another man in black tie. Good, her brother could take over some of the work they were meant to share. But as they moved closer she froze. His companion was tall, broad-shouldered, with thick black hair. Something about the way the man held himself caught her attention, and for a crazy, breath-stealing moment she thought it was Finn.

She gave herself a mental shake. *Don't be so ridiculous.*

Was her heart going to jolt every time she saw someone even vaguely resembling the Australian man she was unable to forget? She thought she saw Finn everywhere: getting out of a car on Bond Street in London, striding along the Rue du Faubourg Saint-Honoré in Paris, even on the streets of the Montovian business capital, St Pierre.

Of course it was never him—never the man she wanted. When they turned around they didn't resemble him at all and she felt deflated and embarrassed.

Finn had become an obsession.

And now her feverish imaginings had conjured up a phantom Finn, right here in the palace.

She headed towards Tristan, just to be sure. Tristan's companion, as if he'd sensed her gaze on him, turned around to face her.

Him!

Natalia had to grab on to the plinth of a nearby piece of priceless sculpture—irreplaceable if it wobbled and fell. She didn't care. She had to anchor herself or she might slide into a faint. She felt light-headed, dizzy, overwhelmed by a wave of sheer joy and exultation.

Finn. It was really him. There could be no mistaking his dark good looks.

Finn. Here in Montovia.

It was as if all her hopes and dreams of the last three months had materialised into six foot two of solid, handsome Australian male. Had he discovered who she was? Come after her? Had he longed for her as she'd longed for him?

Panic tore through her like a whirlwind. What could she possibly say that would make sense after the way they had parted? She had treated him with unforgivable rudeness, leading him

KANDY SHEPHERD   89

on, standing him up and then disappearing. She wanted to throw herself into his arms and thank him for seeking her out. Apologise. Beg his forgiveness. *Grovel.*

He looked over and caught her eye. She attempted a smile, but it was as if her mouth had had enough of smiling that evening and she could only manage something that was more grimace than grin. His expression in return was polite, restrained—the kind of look she often saw on the faces of strangers in such a social situation, when commoners encountered royalty.

Her mouth went dry. All this angst for nothing. *He didn't recognise her.*

Finn guessed the elegant dark-haired woman in the glamorous gown must be Tristan's sister, Princess Natalia. He was predisposed not to like her. Irrational, he knew, but the name was too uncomfortably close to the name of the girl who had so cruelly played him in Sydney and left him high and dry.

Tristan confirmed his guess as to the woman's identity. 'Come and meet my sister,' he said now, with an amused sideways glance that Finn did not understand.

'With pleasure,' Finn said, letting Tristan guide him across the room.

When he'd made fun of Eliza having a real-life

prince at her wedding, he'd never imagined he would end up doing business with him. Or that he'd *like* the guy. He'd been briefly introduced to Tristan at the wedding, and then had been surprised to be contacted by him when Tristan was renegotiating the contract for the distribution of Montovia's renowned chocolate and cheeses into Australia, New Zealand and the Pacific region.

Finn had won the lucrative contract. He had also proposed to Tristan that he work with one of his other clients to develop a prestige Montovian chocolate liqueur. Tristan had been very taken with the idea and had invited Finn to visit his kingdom.

He'd flown in that morning via London, to the small town of Montovia, which took its name from the country. Stepping off the plane had been like stepping through a portal to a totally different world. The place was like something from a movie, where witches and wizards might suddenly appear. A fortified medieval castle was perched high on a mountainside above a lake, looking down on cobbled streets, gingerbread-style houses and the spire of an ancient cathedral. And now here he was, inside the grand stateroom of the glittering palace that Tristan and his family called home.

The Princess waited regally for them to approach—as, Finn supposed, a princess would. She was lovely—very slender, with dark hair twisted off her face in a severe up-do, as befitted the formality of the evening. She didn't smile, rather she looked serious, perhaps somewhat snotty. Again, he supposed that might be typical princess behaviour. But she did manage a tentative hint of a smile.

He frowned, chasing a memory. There was something familiar about her smile... But then the smile was gone, and so was his moment of fleeting recognition.

As he approached she held out her hand—pale, slender, with perfectly manicured nails. He hesitated. Was he meant to kiss it? Bow down before her? No. It appeared that a formal handshake was all that was required.

'My sister, the Princess Natalia,' Tristan said.

'Finn O'Neill,' Finn said in turn.

He took the Princess's hand in a firm grip and was surprised to find it trembled. How could she possibly be nervous? She must shake many strangers' hands on occasions like this.

Tristan briefly explained his business connection with Finn. 'You two might have already met,' he said, looking from one to the other.

Huh? No way would he have forgotten meeting a beautiful young princess. 'I don't believe so,' he said.

The Princess's long pause began to seem awkward. Did she speak English? Because he sure as hell didn't know a word of Montovian.

She cleared her throat, gave a little cough before finally she spoke. 'Hello, Finn,' she said. 'I... I'm as shocked to see you here as you must be to see me.'

Her English-accented voice was immediately familiar, and plunged him back into a million memories of the enchantress back in Sydney who had made an utter fool of him. The woman who had bailed on him without a goodbye or any word of explanation.

He seethed at the mere thought of her. Maybe he really had fallen into a place populated by witches and warlocks, because *this* woman was claiming to be *that* woman and it could not possibly be true.

He decided to test her. 'Natalie Gerard?'

The Princess bit her bottom lip, avoided his gaze. 'There's actually no such person. But I called myself that when I was in Sydney. When... when we met at Eliza and Jake's wedding. I was incognito and in disguise.'

Finn stared at the woman who stood before him in the glittering dark dress. *This was not the person he had known in Sydney.* Natalie had long, thick blonde hair. Princess Natalia's hair was dark, almost black, and put up in that severe style. Natalie was curvaceous; Natalia was very slender. She wore an elegant, modest gown; the last time he'd seen Natalie she'd been wearing only her pink lace underwear.

Hell, Natalia was an uptight Montovian princess, who lived a life of immense privilege in a lavishly appointed palace. Natalie was a sexy, uninhibited English girl on vacation in Sydney, who had made him laugh and been out-and-out naughty. *This was crazy.*

And yet there was something hauntingly familiar about the expressions that flitted across her face.

'I don't believe you're Natalie. Are you her sister? Her cousin?'

This must be some kind of scam. Or real witchy stuff.

'No.' Princess Natalia's dark eyelashes fluttered and her lips curved in a tremulous smile, as if that was the most ridiculous of suggestions.

Natalie's smile.

The same curving of lush, beautifully shaped lips…the same perfect white teeth. Yet the smile seemed subdued, of lower wattage, not lit by the vivacity of Natalie. Finn looked closer, not caring that the intensity of his examination might breach some royal protocol. The eyes. Those beautiful iris-blue eyes.

He glanced back to Tristan. Not that he was in the habit of staring into another guy's eyes but, yes, they were the same blue, just a shade darker than his sister's. That was where he'd seen that colour before—when he'd been briefly introduced to Tristan at the wedding. Before the beautiful stranger across the aisle had captivated his attention.

'I really am Natalie,' the Princess said. 'We sat at the same table. We...we swapped the place cards.'

'You danced with my sister,' said Tristan. 'More than once.'

He'd done a whole lot more than dance with Natalie Gerard. But this woman? *He didn't know her.*

An older man in military uniform passing by caught Tristan's eye and he turned to acknowledge him. In the moment when Tristan was distracted, the Princess stepped closer.

'Don't you remember? You were my tutor in living dangerously,' she whispered.

Only Natalie could know that.

Finn reeled, shocked not just by the intimacy of her words but by her closeness, her floral scent—so achingly familiar that it jolted him with memories he had battled to suppress.

Tristan turned his attention back to them. The Princess rolled her eyes so only Finn could see and in a flash she was the mischievous Natalie he'd known.

What the hell...?

Natalie and Princess Natalia were like light and shade. Yet the more he looked at the Princess, the more he could see Natalie. Until they morphed into one and the same person. Was she a natural blonde or a natural brunette? Her deception sickened him.

He clenched his fists by his sides. 'I can't get my head around this. Why the disguise? Why the deception?'

'It was the only way I was allowed to go to Eliza and Jake's wedding and get a chance to see Sydney. If the media had known I was there, it might have deflected attention from the bride and groom.'

'Why would the media be so interested in *you*?'

She flushed. 'Because I—'

Tristan interjected. 'Because she is a beautiful European princess who isn't yet married. That's reason enough for their interest.'

'Did Eliza know who you were?' he asked. Then he answered his own question. 'Of course she does. She warned me off Natalie Gerard. Now I see why.'

Princess Natalia's eyebrows rose—they were black, Natalie's had been light brown. 'What did she say about me? Eliza and the other Party Queens were sworn to secrecy.'

'Eliza did not betray your trust,' he said, tight-lipped.

How right Eliza had been to try and steer him away from Natalie out of concern for him. That beautiful girl in the pink lace dress had been a liar and a fraud. And he'd been fool enough to have been taken in by her.

He cringed when he remembered how fascinated he had been by her. How genuine she had seemed. How achingly he'd wanted her. How he'd started to wonder if she could be more than a fling.

'My sister's escapade in Sydney must be kept a secret,' Tristan said. 'No one must know about her time pretending to be a commoner.'

A commoner? Who used such terms in this day and age? A hereditary prince like Tristan, Finn thought grimly. And a hereditary princess like his sister. A woman who had made a game out of slumming it with the commoners in Sydney.

He was her dirty little secret.

'I would appreciate it if you kept that confidence now we are doing business together.'

Finn didn't miss the warning in the Crown Prince's words, or the appeal in the Princess's eyes. The Montovian deal was both lucrative and prestigious. He didn't want to jeopardise it.

'I won't spill any beans,' he said through gritted teeth.

This situation was utterly unreal. As if he was trapped in a dark spider's web.

'I appreciate your discretion,' said Tristan. 'I didn't make the connection with the man Natalia was dancing with and the owner of one of the biggest food import and export companies in Australia until I actually met you face to face.'

'Your sister looked very different then. I really didn't recognise her.'

He wanted to tell Tristan's duplicitous sister exactly what he thought of her. Which would hardly be appropriate, considering their surroundings. He took a breath to steady himself. Inhaled that exciting Natalie scent. Wanted to spit it out.

'My sister did a good job in keeping under the radar,' Tristan said.

'I was under strict orders not to let anyone know who I really was,' she said, with an undertone of pleading in her voice. 'There are three important rules a Montovian princess must follow: she must never attract attention for the wrong reason, never be the focus of critical press and never be seen to reflect badly on the throne.' She paused. 'Of course there are a whole lot of other rules too.'

'And by following those rules she enjoyed her vacation and avoided any scandal,' said Tristan, looking approvingly at his sister.

Tristan obviously had no clue that he and Natalie had done much more than chat and dance. Finn suspected that in Tristan's eyes her behaviour on the evening of the wedding would have been considered highly scandalous for a princess.

He remembered how passionate she had been. How intrigued he'd been by her. How gutted he'd been when he'd gone to the hotel the next morning to find she'd checked out and left no forwarding address. How furious.

She'd made a total fool of him. He wanted nothing to do with Natalie/Natalia. Yet his glance kept returning to her, and he was fascinated that this woman was the same one who had enchanted him in Sydney. She was, without a doubt, a mistress of disguise, totally without scruples—and a very good liar.

She looked up at him with those beautiful blue eyes that could lie and lie and lie. 'Finn, I'm sorry I wasn't honest with you. I had no choice.'

Everyone *always* had a choice whether to tell the truth or lie. He wanted to explain that to her. But in the interests of diplomacy and doing business with her family he could only nod tersely. Her behaviour had been unforgivable. The sooner he could turn on his heel and walk away from her, the better. That was if he was allowed to turn his back on her. He was a 'commoner' and she was royalty. Perhaps she expected him to walk backwards from her presence, bowing and scraping all the way.

No matter how lucrative the Montovian contract, he would never, ever agree to do that.

Tristan didn't seem aware of the tension between him and his sister. 'It is good that you two have reconnected,' he said. 'Because unfortunately an emergency calls me away from here tomorrow. Natalia, can I ask you, please, to stand in for me in my meetings with Finn?'

The Princess looked as disconcerted as Finn felt. 'What meetings?' she said.

'Tomorrow morning I have organised a meeting for Finn with our master chocolatier at the chocolate factory.'

'That's always a pleasure,' she said.

'And then a meeting with the Chocolate Makers' Association over lunch.'

She nodded. 'You will need to brief me on the agenda.'

Tristan turned to Finn. 'Natalia has her own interests, with her auctions and other charity work, but she also keeps her finger on the bigger picture of Montovia's trade interests, and works with me when required.'

What choice did Finn have but to agree? 'Fine by me,' he said.

'Natalia is also an expert on the castle and the old town. Natalia, could you please give Finn a tour of the castle in the morning and the points of interest in the town in the afternoon?'

'Of course,' she said.

Tristan gave a slight bow. 'I must attend to my other guests. I shall leave you to carry on your conversation. Finn will be our guest for three days. There will be other opportunities for us to introduce him to our beautiful country during that time.'

CHAPTER SIX

NATALIA HAD TO keep shooting glances at Finn to make sure he was real—actually here in Montovia, working with her brother, and now with her, to further her country's interests.

She wanted to reach up and touch him, to check he was indeed solid flesh and blood and not some hallucination she had conjured up out of her hopeless longing for him. But she didn't dare risk it—not a hand on his arm, not a finger trailed down the smooth olive skin of his cheek. She had seen Finn's eyes frost with cold disdain when he'd realised the truth of who she was, how she'd deceived him. Her touch would no longer be welcomed.

After Tristan had headed off towards another guest and left her alone with Finn, his expression didn't warm into anything less forbidding. Yet for all the shock of encountering him so unexpectedly, and his open hostility—for which she couldn't blame him—she felt an effervescent joy bubble through her. She'd thought she would never see him again anywhere but in her dreams. It was like some kind of magic that he was here, just touching distance away.

Finn. The strong attraction that had made every

other man in the room—in the world—disappear
from her awareness had not been dispersed by
three months of absence. And now Tristan had
delivered Finn back to her.

Soon they would be called to dinner. It was unlikely she would be seated near him. And there
could be no mischievous swapping of place cards
at a palace soirée. She felt an urgent need to apologise, to explain, to try and salvage something of
that memorable time with him in Sydney. But she
did not want to be overheard.

'Finn,' she said in a low voice. 'I don't think
we need an audience. Shall we move over to that
corner of the room?'

He nodded and followed her away from the
main body of guests towards the windows that
looked over the lake, closed to the chilly Novem-
ber evening. It was only a few steps away but it
gave them some breathing space without being
so private that her tête-à-tête with a handsome
man would give rise to gossip.

The heavy gold brocade curtains had been
pulled back to give a dramatic view across the
lake, with the full moon reflected in the dark
water, gleaming on the permanent snow high on
the jagged peaks of the mountains. Finn admired
the view with what seemed like genuine appreciation. In other circumstances it would have been
romantic.

But romance was, sadly, not on the agenda. This was more akin to a confrontation.

An uncomfortable silence fell between them. Finn was the first to break it. 'I keep telling myself there must be a rational explanation for your deception,' he said.

'Rational?' She took a deep intake of breath. 'There was nothing rational about how I felt about you,' she said in a voice that wasn't quite steady.

He frowned. 'What do you mean?'

'Meeting you in Sydney was so unexpected and…and wonderful. I had never felt like that about a man. I told you—you made the wedding magic for me. Logically, I should have said goodnight when the wedding wound up. But I simply couldn't bear to shake your hand and thank you for your company as I should have. I was desperate to cling on to every possible minute with you. But I had given my word not to reveal my identity to anyone.' She hesitated. 'Also, I wondered if you would treat me the same way if you knew who I really was.'

'That was my decision to make,' he said. 'You didn't give me the opportunity to make it. Yet you trusted others with the truth.'

'I didn't know you. I had to be cautious. You could have been a reporter for all I knew.'

But she had trusted him enough to want to

make love with him. And had spent the last three months regretting that caution had kicked in.

'I trusted you to be who you said you were. But it was just a game to you.'

'No. It wasn't a game. I… I really liked you.'

But she hadn't been honest with him. *'Alla prossima,'* he had murmured, and she had translated, knowing it was a lie, that they would not meet again. Since then she had had plenty of opportunity to reflect on how he must have felt when he'd discovered she had gone without any explanation or goodbye.

She looked up at him, registered the shock he must have felt on seeing *her*, not the Natalie he had known. Maybe she had done too good a job on that disguise if he was having such difficulty reconciling the two aspects of her.

She tried to make all the regret she felt for treating him so thoughtlessly show in her eyes. 'Finn. I'm sorry for—'

His dark brows drew together. 'Sorry for what? Choose an option for your apology—you have several.'

He held up his left hand and ticked off her options finger by finger with his right hand. *Beautiful hands that had felt so good on her body.*

'Option one—lying so thoroughly about your identity. Option two—standing me up by disappearing off the face of the earth with no explanation. Option three—making me go through that charade just now of guessing your identity.'

She swallowed hard against a lump of anguish. He thought so badly of her. 'I… I plead guilty to options one and two, but I'm innocent of option three,' she said. 'I expect you must be angry, but you can't pin that one on me.'

'Did you really not know I'd be here tonight? Or was that another game for the amusement of you and your brother?'

'I had absolutely no idea you would be here. Tristan had not informed me. I was so shocked I thought I was going to faint.'

His mouth twisted into a cynical line she hadn't seen before. 'You understand I might find it difficult to believe a word you say ever again?'

His words hit their target and she flushed. 'I get that,' she said. 'But I really didn't have a clue you would be here tonight—or indeed that Tristan was doing business with you. I don't know why he didn't tell me. Especially as he wants me to attend some of his meetings with our Montovian business people. I can only think he wanted to surprise me because he realised we'd met at the wedding.'

'He certainly surprised *me*,' he said, with a wry twist to his mouth.

'Me too—and I wish he'd told me. Although for me it was a pleasant surprise. I… I'm happy to see you again, Finn, in spite of the way it's happened.' She looked up at him, but his only response was a grudging nod. 'Possibly Tristan thought springing us on each other might be simpler than having to explain who I really was. Remember, he doesn't know about…about what happened after the wedding?'

'Perhaps,' he said—with, she thought, a slight thawing of his frosty demeanour.

'As Crown Prince and heir to the throne, Tristan is working hard to modernise the royal family and some of their really stuffy old ways of doing things. It's a big job and he's getting both Gemma and me involved in it. He's also become an active advocate for our country's exports. I wasn't trained in business, but I'm doing my best to help with the trade side of things.'

Finn frowned. '*He* was trained for it but not you, even as second in line to the throne?'

'It sounds very old fashioned, I know, but I was brought up to make a strategic marriage to a man of noble birth. Tristan studied law. My older brother studied economics. I was sent to a strict Swiss finishing school. However, once I'd graduated, with straight As in deportment and how to manage servants, I insisted I be allowed to follow my own interest and study architecture in London.'

'So there's no career in fashion?'

Again, there was that cynical edge to his voice. Again, she couldn't blame him.

'Well, not in the retail sense. However, I do work very hard on my fashion auctions, so that isn't a total fib.'

'Fashion auctions?'

She was pleased to see genuine interest. 'You haven't heard of them? I don't suppose you would have. As Princess of Montovia, I'm the patron of several charities—including my own favourite, which works with an international foundation to support the education of girls in developing countries. Long story short: a lot of designer clothes and accessories are only worn once or twice by people like me and my privileged friends. As a fundraiser, I organised an online auction of donated items which was so successful it's become a regular thing and it's getting bigger and bigger. We get both donations and bids from all around the world. The charity has really benefitted, way beyond the scope of regular donations.'

'That sounds admirable,' he said.

'I'm proud of it,' she said.

'It seems you should be.' He paused, searched her face. 'I'm still struggling to make sense of you being a princess. For instance, what do I call you? Natalia? Princess? Your Highness? Is bended knee required?'

'Natalia is fine. Or Natalie would work too. I

am Natalie, Finn. Or I was in Sydney, where I was *allowed* to be her.'

She couldn't keep the wistfulness from her voice. It had been a taste of a different life. A bright, flaming light interspersed between various shades of grey, with Finn being the most brilliant of flames.

'Natalie Gerard told me she was single. What about Princess Natalia?'

'Notorious for being single. In spite of a lifetime of grooming for wifedom.'

'Notorious?'

She sighed. 'Now that you know who I am, I'll save you the trouble of looking up media reports about the "Heartbreaker Princess", or the "Bachelor Princess". I make great copy for the European gossip magazines because I've rejected the proposals of six palace-approved men. Actually, seven now. I've knocked back another one since I got home from Australia.'

'Wait. You can't choose your own husband? He has to be approved?'

Put like that, no wonder he sounded incredulous.

'Until recently Montovian royalty could only marry spouses with noble blood.'

'No "commoners" allowed?' he said, using his fingers to make quote marks and his voice to let her know just what he thought of the term.

She realised how insulting the word was. Another anachronism for her and Tristan to work on.

'That's right. But then Tristan used his considerable legal research skills to search the royal archives and discovered that any reigning King could amend that rule. My father was persuaded to change it—the restriction has not made for happy marriages in our family, including that of my parents—so Tristan could marry for love. As it turned out, Gemma discovered she was distantly related to both the English and the Danish royal families, so the change in rule was not needed. I remain somewhat of a test case.'

'So you're allowed to marry who you want to?'

'In theory, yes. In practice, my parents still want me to marry a well-born European aristocrat. In fact, they have to give their permission, whoever I might want to marry. I am, after all, second in line to the throne. You may not know that my older brother Carl was…was killed in a helicopter crash, along with his wife and two-year-old son.'

Her voice hitched. It was still so difficult to talk about the accident, even to acknowledge that it had happened. She didn't think she would ever get over the loss of the brother she'd adored, his precious little son Rudi, or poor Sylvie, too young to die. One day Carl had been there, acting the bossy big brother, and the next he'd been gone. She didn't think she'd ever be able to come to terms with it.

'I'm sorry. I did read about the tragedy in my research on Montovia.'

Natalia took a moment to collect herself. 'Everything changed. Losing Carl meant I moved up to second in line to the throne. And Tristan had been quite the party boy until then. He had to step up to the responsibility of being Crown Prince and the future King. My parents threw a cordon of protection around me. Suddenly it seemed as though I'd been thrown back to the nursery.'

'If that was the case, how were you allowed to swan around Sydney by yourself?'

She shrugged. 'I wasn't. I could pretend I had absolute freedom, but my bodyguards were always close to hand.'

His dark brows rose. 'Your bodyguards?'

She nodded. 'That waiter at the wedding who was hovering solicitously nearby?'

'I thought he fancied you.'

She shook her head. 'Just doing his job. As was the chauffeur of the hire car. Both Montovian bodyguards.'

Finn ran his ran through his hair. Natalia ached to smooth it down for him but didn't dare. She wasn't sure what kind of reception she'd get.

'And at your hotel?'

yours, for that matter. You've apologised.
t it behind me.'

ee,' she said, feeling as though she had lost
er something of immeasurable value.

he saw from the set of his jaw that Finn the
nessman had taken over.

That's as far as it goes,' he said. 'There's noth-
g in the contract I've signed with your brother
hat necessitates me spending extended time with
ou. The business meetings are necessary, but
there's no need for the guided tour. I just want
to finalise my business with Tristan and get the
hell out of here.'

Mutely, she nodded. 'Of course,' she finally
managed to choke out.

She looked up at him and recognised the mar-
vellous man she had connected with in Sydney.
Finn. Every moment she had spent with him was
seared on her memory. But he looked at her and
didn't see Natalie. He saw a stranger who had
lied to him, who had made a fool of him. She
had hurt him. And he didn't want anything further to do with her.

She was in a room filled with other people, and
the murmur of conversation was rising and falling around her, yet she had never felt so alone.

Finn felt bad at the Princess's shocked expression.
There was hurt there, too, in those beautiful blue

'They shared the adjoining room.'

Finn's disbelief and horror was to be expected.
'You mean they could hear what was going on in
your room?'

'Probably.'

She couldn't meet his eyes. She had asked her
bodyguards not to mention that she'd had a visitor
to her hotel room. They liked her. She sometimes
thought they felt sorry for her, for the restricted
life she had to live in spite of her wealth and privilege. There had been no adverse reports back to
her parents. As far as they had observed it had
been entirely innocent.

He swore under his breath. 'It just gets worse.'

'What do you mean?'

'My recollection of that day is vastly different
from yours. It's like we were operating on two
different levels of reality.'

'I'm still *me*, Finn.'

He shook his head. 'I don't know you, Princess
Natalia.' He made a credible attempt at a bow. 'I
knew Natalie. I liked Natalie a lot. She was gorgeous and she was fun. Things moved fast with
me and Natalie—until she put on the brakes. That
was frustrating, but it was her prerogative. We
arranged to meet the next day and I went away
a happy man. Then I turned up at her hotel, to
take her sailing as arranged. Only to find she had
checked out very early that morning. She didn't

leave me a message at the desk to explain. No. She just disappeared. Standing there in that lobby, when I realised I'd been stood up in a spectacular manner, wasn't my finest moment.'

She cringed at the pain on his face. 'I really am sorry, but I can explain—'

'Can you?' He shrugged. 'After I got over my annoyance—and I admit my intense disappointment—I figured Natalie was a tourist, looking for some no-strings fun. She ran out of time and ran out of town. I'd been played. I should have known better.'

She gasped. 'It really wasn't like that.'

But that was how it must have appeared…

'So, what's *your* version of events?'

She shifted from one stilettoed foot to the other. 'I… I couldn't bear to say goodbye for real. I was scared I would break down and spill the truth about myself. Which would have got me into big trouble. I know I'm twenty-seven years old, but my parents aren't just my parents. They're the King and Queen of my country and their word is law. Our private jet was there to take me home with Tristan and Gemma. I was obligated to go with them. I wanted to part on good terms with you. So I didn't tell you I was leaving. It…made it easier.'

She closed her eyes at the image of Finn ask-

ing at the hotel reception told she'd gone. How must

'Your definition of parting seems to translate as leaving piled upon lie.'

'Guilty as charged,' she said, feel ibly sad.

She couldn't tell him about all that vated her without giving away her enti She was still a virgin. Her situation changed. To make love with him would come with risks and consequences that had changed in the three months since she'd kissed him goodbye at the door of her hotel room. Maybe now she might take those risks on board if she got the chance, but maybe duty would still win out.

She realised she could apologise all she wanted for the Natalie Gerard deception, but he would never forget what she'd done.

He would never again believe a word she said.

He looked down into her face, as if searching it for the answers he might sense she wasn't giving.

'Loss of face is important to me. You made me look foolish. Not to mention gutted at losing Natalie, who had made quite an impact on me.' He paused, took a step back from her. His expression hardened. 'But what happened in Sydney wasn't really that significant. It wasn't even a day of my

eyes. But he could only get his head around this very odd situation he found himself plunged into by thinking of Natalia as someone he didn't know.

She wasn't the woman he had fallen for in Sydney. Not fallen *in love* with. Of course not. For one thing, he was not a believer in love at first sight—he'd confused infatuation with love with Chiara. But his meeting with the woman he'd known as Natalie Gerard had been something bigger than just a casual hook-up at a wedding.

The fact she lived in another country had been cause enough for him to put the brakes on. However, his time with her had come skidding to an abrupt halt before he'd even had a chance to think about the wisdom of taking things further. This woman—Princess Natalia—was absolutely out of bounds in too many ways to count.

It wasn't just that she lived on the other side of the world from him, hers was a world where he was considered a 'commoner', lacking in status or authority. How could trying to rekindle those Sydney feelings go anywhere? For him a serious relationship—one day perhaps marriage—was all about a partnership of equals, working together to enjoy life together and then, when the time was right, raising a family. Like his parents, his grandparents, his friends like Eliza and Jake.

The sooner he put Natalie/Natalia behind him, the better.

He followed her to the football-stadium-sized dining room, noting the sexy swing of her hips. The sway was not quite the same as the one he'd seen before from her alter ego, as the Princess was wearing a restrictive long gown, but it was every bit as enticing.

He was still having difficulty getting his head around the fact she was 100 per cent Natalie, but the sway when she walked was undeniably hers. The way she'd looked so different in Sydney was a kind of witchery, a modern sleight of hand, magic performed by hairdressers and make-up artists and a princess who was a mistress of the art of dissembling.

The grand Montovian royal dining room, with its soaring moulded ceilings, was decorated like a museum, with priceless antiques, masterpieces on the walls, crystal chandeliers and gleaming gold place settings. Very formal…very European. Wealth beyond the bounds of imagination.

He was not seated next to Natalia, for which he was thankful. He had no desire to revive memories of the last time they had shared a table. It hurt too much to remember how happy he'd been in her company.

Man, had that Kerry woman got her predictions wrong. Her so-called psychic powers hadn't picked up on a false identity.

Princess Natalia was seated on the opposite

side of the table. Close enough so he could observe her, not close enough to talk to her. She was so elegant, so poised, her smile so charming. The lights picked up the diamonds glittering at her ears and her wrists. A real princess. Yet she seemed subdued—as if someone had dimmed the lights on Natalie to result in Natalia.

He noticed she pushed the food around on her plate with her fork, scarcely a bite reaching her mouth. It wasn't the fault of the food, which was superb. No wonder she was so slender. Natalie had had a hearty appetite.

He would go crazy if he kept comparing them.

His mind finally grasped the fact that Natalia was indeed Natalie, but she seemed like a diminished version of the woman he'd met in Sydney.

He was seated near Tristan, alongside his cousin Marco and his wife Amelie. Over dinner, they talked about their time in the Montovian military, where service was compulsory for all young people.

Tristan had served, despite his royal status, and Marco—a count and high-ranking officer—had met his doctor wife Amelie—a Montovian commoner—while deployed on a peace-keeping force in an African country. They had only been able to marry because of the change in law Tristan had brought about.

It was such a different world to the one Finn had experienced growing up. Again he had the sense that he had fallen into a movie set. Perhaps even a different century.

Just before dessert was to be served, Finn found himself in private conversation with Tristan.

'Natalia tells me you have politely turned down her services as tour guide,' Tristan said.

'Yes, I have to catch up on some work between meetings.' It was as polite an excuse as he'd been able to come up with on the spot.

'Would you consider changing your mind?' Tristan asked.

The guy was a prince and Finn was a guest in his palace. Was this a lightly veiled order?

'I suppose I could…' he said slowly, not certain where this would take him.

'I would appreciate it if you'd spend that extra time with her,' Tristan said. 'You see, we're worried about Natalia. All the family have expressed their concern.'

'Concern?'

Tristan sighed. 'She is not herself since she returned from Australia. Almost as if she has disengaged from her life in the palace. She does her duty—Natalia is nothing if not dutiful—but she's lacking in zest, showing no real enthusiasm for anything, except perhaps her auctions. That's not like her at all. You must have noticed how thin she has become? That is in spite of Gemma organising special meals to tempt her appetite.'

An unexpected terror struck Finn's heart. 'You think she's unwell?' He choked out the words.

Her lies, the deception, his loss of face—all seemed suddenly insignificant now he was faced with the possible loss of this woman who had moved him to the edge of both love and hate.

'Perhaps… I don't know. I can't ask her doctor. Even the Crown Prince can't do that. My sister is an independent person.'

'But how do you think spending more time with me would help?'

'It has struck me that the last time I saw my sister laugh was when she was dancing with you at Eliza's wedding in Sydney. Perhaps you can make her laugh again?'

CHAPTER SEVEN

FINN HAD ARRANGED to meet Natalia, via an exchange of stilted phone conversations, early the next morning at the high, locked wooden gate that opened on to some stone steps leading up to the external walkways and corridors of the castle. As he approached he could see she was already there, her back to him, looking out to the lake below.

She was dressed in sombre colours: dark grey trousers, black boots, a thick wool light-grey jacket, a silver-coloured scarf. Her dark hair swung straight and loose to skim her shoulders, gleaming in the mid-morning sunlight.

Against the backdrop of the towering walls of the castle, the vastness of the lake, she seemed fragile and alone, and Finn remembered Tristan's concern. He thought about his own realisation that she might be suffering from depression, and felt a surge of remorse at how harshly he'd spoken to her the previous day, when she had tried so hard to be honest with him.

She needed kindness and understanding, not condemnation. He needed to tell her that. Explain his perhaps over-the-top reaction to the startling news about her identity. Make his own apologies.

As he walked towards her his shoes crunched on the crushed stone pathway. 'Natalia!' he called.

Startled, she turned to face him.

Her first expression on catching sight of him was, to his immense surprise, delight—quickly covered by a schooled indifference. She was aloof, but not in the manner of a princess—rather in the manner of a woman who had been told that the passion she'd shared was of no importance, easily forgotten.

Inwardly, Finn cursed himself for his thoughtlessness. And his dishonesty. He hadn't meant a word of it. He'd used those words to hide his battered pride and hurt that she had walked out on him without notice.

'You called me Natalia,' she said, after he'd reached her and stood hand-shaking distance apart.

'Yes,' he said. 'There's no point in arguing over semantics. Natalia is your given name. Natalie is the anglicised version of your name. I have a Chinese name—Ming-tun—which only my grandfather uses. What I'm trying to say is the name doesn't matter. It's the person.'

'Thank you,' she said. 'I like Ming-tun. What does it mean?'

Her cheeks were flushed pink with the cold and her eyes shone blue. She was every bit as lovely as a brunette as she had been as a blonde.

'It means intelligent. My grandfather had high hopes.'

'Seems to me you've lived up to your name. He must be proud.'

'I've done my best,' he said.

But how intelligently had he dealt with the revelation of her real identity?

He had studied hard at school and at university because it had been expected of him. His immigrant grandparents and father set great store on a good education. But all he'd ever wanted to do was to dive head-first into the family business. Although without his degree perhaps he would not have been able to drive the business forward so successfully, so quickly.

She looked up at him, her head tilted to one side, blue eyes narrowed. 'What made you change your mind?'

'About your name? I decided it was pointless thinking of you as two different people when Natalia and Natalie are one and the same.'

'I didn't mean that. I meant you being here this morning. Last night, you seemed so sure you didn't want me to show you around. You said that we would meet at the chocolate factory.'

It's because your family are concerned you're depressed and it shocked me.

Tristan hadn't exactly said that, but his concerns about Natalia had immediately raised flags for Finn. One of his mates in high school had had an undiagnosed depression that had ended in a funeral after he had taken his own life. Finn had beaten himself up for not having been there for his friend.

His school had insisted that the boy's classmates attend extensive counselling, and ever since he'd been alert for symptoms of depression in the people close to him. He'd been able to get help for them when he'd seen the signs. He'd recognised them in Tristan's description of Natalia.

'Why did I change my mind? Perhaps the fact I don't speak a word of Montovian?' It wasn't the world's best excuse but he decided to run with it. 'Your cousin Marco warned me that many of the townsfolk don't feel comfortable speaking English, even though they study it in school, and that Montovian is a language almost impossible for a foreigner to learn.'

'It *is* a difficult language,' she said. 'However, Gemma is becoming fluent in it so it can be mastered. But that doesn't really answer my question.'

He squirmed just a little under the gaze of those perceptive blue eyes. 'I guess it doesn't,' he said. 'Truth is, I realised I'd be crazy to knock back the services of a guide who's a member of the royal family, who must know so much about Montovia.'

'It's true we've been around for centuries,' she said drily.

'That's exactly my point,' he said.

'I appreciate your worthy explanation, Finn. But I suspect the real truth is that Tristan coerced you into it.'

'Not true.'

She raised her dark eyebrows. 'Really?'

'Well, possibly true. Not coerced. He asked me to reconsider. He's concerned about you. Thinks you're unhappy. He thought I might be able to cheer you up. That I seemed to have the touch.'

She smiled—a slow, curving smile that was a ghost of her usual dazzling smile but still very appealing, with a hint of sensuality. He realised that she was remembering, as he was, just how he had kept her entertained back in Sydney.

'Tristan has no idea about you and me at the wedding, does he?' she said.

'Not a clue,' he said. 'He and Gemma left before the end, I believe.'

'So he didn't see us kissing behind the orchids and no one reported it to him, either. Gemma has certainly never mentioned it.'

Memories of the incident flooded his mind. How wonderful she'd felt in his arms. Her scent. Her taste. How sensual and exciting her kisses had been.

How much he'd wanted her.

'We were discreet,' he said, his voice suddenly husky as he looked down into her face.

'Fortunately for us they were very big plant-
ers of orchids.'

As they shared the moment of complicity her
lips parted without her seeming to realise they
were doing it, or that it looked like an invitation
to kiss her again.

'How could I forget?' he said, wrenching his
gaze away from her lips. He knew she knew he
wasn't talking about the orchids.

'If Tristan knew—if my father knew—that you
had come back to my hotel room, you would be
languishing in the dungeons right now.'

He wasn't sure if she was joking or not. Not
in this movie set of a home of hers. 'You have
dungeons?'

'They're not part of my guided tour, but, yes.
Genuine dungeons—damp, dreary and complete
with medieval instruments of torture.'

'Don't tell me—some of them are specifically
designed for men who compromise the virtue of
Montovian princesses?'

'Indeed,' she said, with a hint of that mischief he'd liked so much. 'Custom-made to fit
the crime.'

'*Ouch*. Dancing with a princess in those days
really meant living dangerously.'

He grimaced and she laughed.

He'd made her laugh.

It made him feel good to see her laugh.

'Don't worry too much,' she said. 'The torture chambers are intact but they haven't been used for a long, long time.'

'Still, it might be wise to keep Tristan in ignorance about the extent of our time together in Sydney,' he said.

'Yes. He obviously likes you and trusts you. I don't believe he'd want to torture you just to defend the honour of his sister.'

'I sincerely hope not, if we're to do business together. He saw that you enjoyed dancing with me—that's all he needs to know.' He paused, not sure how far he should go in case she clammed up. 'He tells me he hasn't noticed you enjoying yourself much since.'

All traces of laughter vanished. Her mouth set in a tight, unapproachable, distinctly unkissable line. 'That's probably true.'

She went to turn away, and he sensed her closing up on him. 'Natalia…' He put a hand on her shoulder to turn her back to face him, then dropped it immediately when she complied.

There could be no more touching—even through the thickness of a coat. Not now he truly understood the situation. He was careful. They were not completely alone on these battlements. There was a party of gardeners in sight, and no doubt they'd encounter other people.

'Is Tristan right? *Are* you unhappy? I've noticed how different you are from your time in Sydney. It's not just the hair colour—which I like, by the way. But it's as if…as if your light has dimmed.'

'That could be because it's winter.' She didn't quite carry off the light-hearted retort.

'Perhaps…' he said. 'You've lost a lot of weight, too.'

'Isn't there an old saying that you can never be too rich or too thin?'

'If you want to be thin, that's okay. But you do seem different. Not as vivacious.'

She closed her eyes tight for a moment, as if to give herself time to think. Or to look back into her past.

'I wasn't happy before I went to Australia. My personal life didn't seem to be my own any more. Not since Carl died and everything changed. That's why I wanted so desperately to go there. To be anonymous. To maybe find what was missing.'

She sighed—a sad sound that struck at Finn's heart. He wanted to take her in his arms to comfort her, but thought better of it.

'You saw me at my best. I was riding a high. I loved the independence and the freedom to be myself. Of course it all came crashing down around me when I got back home.'

'Did you seek any help to deal with that crash? Because—'

She put up her hand in an imperious gesture to stop him from going any further. 'I don't want you feeling sorry for me, Finn. Because there's nothing to be sorry about. And I don't need help.'

'I don't feel sorry for you at all. I'm just concerned.'

She took a deep breath. 'That's very sweet of you. But I can deal with my…my unhappiness.'

'In other words—"butt out, Finn"?'

'Exactly.'

Finn detected the wobble of her lower lip and realised she might not be as composed as she wanted him to believe.

'I know I'm the girl who has everything. And I'm not ungrateful. But I'm nearly twenty-eight and I don't have my own life. No career—though the auctions have become a real interest. No husband. No children. Everything is about duty and doing the right thing by others. Marrying for the sake of the succession—not for my own happiness.'

'Would your family honestly force you into marrying someone you didn't like?'

He'd been presented to her parents the night before—King Gerard and Queen Truda. They'd seemed more modern and approachable than he'd imagined.

'*Like* being the operative word. *Love* doesn't come into it—and I won't settle for less than love. Tristan and Gemma have set the standard. My own parents have a miserable marriage. My father wasn't allowed to marry his girlfriend—a girl from a good Montovian family but not good enough for a future king. He put off marriage for as long as he could so he could be with her. Then he had to marry my much younger mother. She thought she was marrying for love—until she was sadly disillusioned by finding out that my father had kept his real love as his mistress and still does to this day. After my mother bore my father a male "heir and a spare", and then me, she was free to do what she wanted so long as she fulfilled her ceremonial duties as Queen when required. She was discreet about the lovers she took. And I think my grandmother actually *hated* my grandfather. Theirs was another marriage of convenience. She subjugated her misery into worthy causes.'

'And you were expected to do the same?'

'Until Tristan had the law changed. Before that I just kept saying no.'

'That was brave of you.'

'It wasn't difficult as none of the men appealed in the slightest. I wouldn't even have answered their posts on a dating site, we had so little in common—not to mention a total lack of chemistry. There was only one man who tempted me. He was good-looking, fun, my own age… I thought we might be able to make a go of an arranged marriage. Until I realised the love of his life was his very handsome private secretary—a charming guy.'

'I'm sorry,' he said, not sure what else to say.

'I needed an escape. Australia seemed to offer it. The whole Natalie thing was an adventure and the freedom was exhilarating.' She dropped both her gaze and her voice, scuffed the pathway with the toe of her boot. 'And then there was you. I... I wasn't expecting you.'

'I wasn't expecting you either,' he said. 'But there you were.'

He remembered standing respectfully, watching the wedding ceremony, and then feeling compelled to turn towards the beautiful woman on the other side of the aisle. After that he'd been unable to think of anything but her.

'I... I'd never been so attracted to someone. I didn't know how to handle it,' she said.

'It *was* powerful. The attraction came from out of the blue for me too. And then we hit it off. You were such fun. It wasn't just about how beautiful you were—*are*—it was the way we seemed to click.'

She looked up at him again. 'It was a first for me.' Her eyes were clouded with bewilderment and loss. 'I'm truly sorry for the way it ended. No wonder you're angry with me.'

He hated to see her hurting. 'Natalia, please… You don't need to say sorry again. Last night I should have made it clear that I accepted your apology for the way you left. Now, even in the short time I've been here in your country, I've got a grasp on the restrictions of your royal life.'

'Thank you. It's difficult to understand if you don't see all this.' She waved her hand to encompass the palace, the castle, the lake and the town below.

'I can also see you were telling the truth when you said you had little control over the situation in Sydney—why you acted the way you did.'

'I had to do the right thing. It was agony, watching you walk away, knowing I would never see you again. I can't imagine you believed that at the time, but it's true. I pretended I was ill all the way home on the plane so I didn't have to talk to Gemma and Tristan.'

'I searched for you. But I—'

Just then a buzzer went off on her watch. Startled, Natalia looked down at it. 'Where did the time go? Our window of opportunity for sightseeing is rapidly shrinking. Soon we need to head out to the chocolate factory.'

He wanted to say that the only sight he wanted to see was her, but knew that would be both cheesy and inappropriate—although true. Despite all his resolve, he found himself falling under her spell again. Only this time he knew who she really was—and that the impediments to any kind of relationship between them were insurmountable.

The girl he'd known as Natalie had said she'd lived in England, and his first thought had been that long-distance couldn't work. But distance seemed nothing compared to the chains of obligation tying Natalia to her life as a royal. At least this time around he knew what he was dealing with.

'Right,' he said. 'Lead on.'

'We won't get much more done this morning than an introduction to the castle. Considering our limited time, I'll take you straight to the walkway on the battlement walls. It has an interesting history and an amazing view.'

'I like the sound of that,' he said.

She paused and eyeballed him. 'It can be cold up there on the battlements. I hope you're dressed warmly enough?'

'These are my northern hemisphere winter clothes,' he said.

He was dressed in the warm cashmere coat, hat and gloves that he only ever wore on his frequent trips to Europe. It never got cold enough in Sydney for them to be taken out of his wardrobe. He didn't think he could bear to live in a cold climate such as this.

The large wrought-iron bolt on the gate slid

open easily. Finn could only imagine the army of staff it took to keep an ancient monument like this in such good order.

As if reading his mind, Natalia paused as she pushed open the gate. 'There's a full-time architect, an engineer, and an army of stonemasons and tradespeople responsible for keeping the castle standing and in such good order. Fact number one—some of these walls that seem so solid are actually stone shells on both sides, filled with rubble. They were designed to withstand contraction and expansion in extreme weather. Imagine— they knew to do that all those years ago.'

'Clever,' he said. 'And getting the stone up the sides of the mountain must have been quite a feat.'

'A system of levers and pulleys, we believe,' she said.

He followed her up several sets of steep, narrow steps, cut into the side of the mountain, until they emerged onto an external corridor that hugged the solid walls of the castle on one side and a high wall on the other.

'Fact number two—'

'You're a really experienced tour guide.'

She laughed. *Laugh number two.*

'Let's just say it's not the first time I've given a visitor a private tour. But this part of the castle is actually open to the public at certain times in the summer.'

'Okay, so hit me with the next fact.'

'The castle was built as a fortress in the eleventh century.'

He whistled. 'That old?'

'Even older. Fact number three—it was built on the ruins of a Roman *castellum*, which was like a watchtower. This was a strategic place for a fortress. The mountains behind form a formidable natural barrier. They were virtually unscalable—especially in winter. Standing on the battlements above us on the lake side they had a clear view of any approaching enemies.'

'You know a lot about it.' He was surprised by her passion for her subject.

'Is it surprising that growing up here I've developed an interest in architecture and a passion for history? Over the centuries the original fortress building was extended to give us the castle we see now.'

'You sound like you've memorised the guide-book,' he said.

'I actually wrote the guidebook,' she said. 'In four different languages.'

'I'm seriously impressed,' he said. 'So tell me more.'

'You're not bored?'

'I'm fascinated.' *As if he could be bored by anything she said.*

'If you're sure?'

He looked down into her face. 'I'm sure,' he said. He didn't intend to say anything further but could not resist adding, 'Sure I've never met a more fascinating woman.'

She blushed high on her cheekbones. 'Thank you.'

'I thought it when we first met and I think it now. I like the way you're so passionate about your heritage.'

'I always have been—ever since I was a child. And as I got older I spent quite a lot of time in the palace archives.'

He could imagine her as a studious little girl and the image was endearing.

'Tell me more about the castle.'

'Fact number four—the south wing, where the palace is, was built not so much as a show of strength but to display the wealth of the royal family.'

'Where wealth equals power of a different kind of strength?'

'Exactly.'

For a moment he might kid himself that she was just a guide, parroting facts from a preset script. But there was no escaping the fact that she was a high-ranking member of the royal family, and that its wealth and power still existed today. Her role brought with it privileges, but also restrictions.

He was beginning to realise what being second in line to the throne actually meant. What it might mean to *him*. If he wanted to see more of her he couldn't just call her and ask her to the movies.

He looked around him with awe. 'The castle is indeed ancient and imposing. To think what these walls must have witnessed over the years…'

'It's mind-boggling, isn't it? This is actually the oldest part of the castle. Let me show you something rather special.'

'The entire place is special,' he said.

'I never take it for granted,' she said 'I love my home and I love my country. It's just that when I was in Sydney I began to wonder if that was enough.'

For a long moment they didn't speak. He looked into her face, trying to read her expression of thoughtful sadness. 'Is that part of your unhappiness?' he asked.

She flushed pinker. 'Yes. No. I really don't know.' She looked down at her watch again. 'But what I *do* know is that we're running out of time. Follow me.'

She stopped just before the path started to widen and put her hand reverently on the thick wall. 'This is what remains of the most heavily barricaded area of the fortress. Fact number five: those slits were where arrows were fired from.'

'No boiling oil dropped down from above?'

One of the computer games he'd enjoyed as a teenager had used that particular device to destroy the enemy. He'd always thought it particularly gruesome.

'That too,' she said, very seriously.

Not just for computer games, then.

'And cannonballs came later.'

'Your ancestors must have been fierce and formidable. And there were the dungeons with the torture chambers too.'

'Exactly.'

They kept walking as the pathway followed the contour of the mountain. It opened up to a lookout comprising several high-arched windows set in a stone wall facing the lake.

'Those arched lookouts came much later than the barricades we just saw. It's always been a popular place.'

Finn stared in wonder at the magnificence of the view framed by the windows. It looked out on not just the vast lake but further, to the system of smaller lakes it adjoined and then the jagged snow-capped mountains reflected in their stillness. Down below, the town, with its cobbled streets, looked like a toy town. The slightest of breezes chased wisps of white cloud across the brilliant blue sky. He found it mind-blowing to think this was her home…her heritage.

'This view is famous,' she said. 'And it's a

favourite for postcards. Now it's famous in the family too, for being the place where Tristan proposed to Gemma. You mustn't repeat that, of course,' she said, putting a warning finger to her lips.

'Another secret for me to keep?' he said.

He realised that the castle and the palace were not just ancient monuments to power and tenacity, the seat of a ruling family dating back centuries, but Natalia's home. And that there would be no place there for a boy from Sydney, no matter how wealthy he might be.

If only Natalia was who she had first appeared to be—an ordinary English girl who could choose what she wanted to do with her life. Someone with whom he could—if he so desired—contemplate a relationship of equals.

Instead he'd met a princess. A woman with loyalties and obligations to the monarchy of which she was part. And that, he suspected, would come before any personal relationship.

It would probably be wise of him to cut his ties with Montovia. Forget the contract with Tristan. Cancel his remaining meetings with the good burghers of the kingdom. Fly home and forget Princess Natalia.

Trouble was, he couldn't forget her. He hadn't forgotten her in the three months between meetings. Possibly he was under some kind of enchantment—he would believe anything in these mythical, medieval surroundings.

The buzzer on Natalia's watch sounded again—a twenty-first century intrusion. She was organised and efficient—something he appreciated.

'Does that mean the tour is over?' he asked.

'Just this part of it,' she said. 'Next on your schedule is our meeting with Franz Schmid, master chocolatier. Montovian chocolate is, as I'm sure you know, a luxury product.'

'The platinum standard of chocolate—that's how I hear it described. The world's best. And that is what interests me about it as a product for import...not just for Australia, but for new markets in Asia.'

'There are a number of chocolate producers in Montovia with whom you'll be dealing, but Franz's business is the largest. It is also very dear to our hearts, as when we were children and started to make official appearances with our parents the chocolate factory was our favourite. Be warned: the scent of chocolate is intoxicating—from the large pods that hold the beans to the pralines and the truffles made from the chocolate butter. And then, of course, there is the taste...'

The chocolate factory was set on the shores of the lake, some miles outside the old town. Behind the façade of a centuries-old stone farmhouse was a small modern factory devoted to the creation of superb chocolate. It was spotless, with the production team—mainly women—wearing white overalls, head-coverings and surgical masks. Although he didn't understand Montovian, Finn could sense the buzz of excitement from the factory floor because the Royal Princess was on the premises.

The chocolatier, Franz, was as jovial as Finn would have expected from someone whose passion was something as delicious as his chocolate. Finn asked lots of questions, as the more he knew about the product the better he could sell it. He wasn't disappointed in the chocolatier's replies about fair trade single-origin cocoa beans, and the use of cream from cows grazing on local pastures. All were part of the story.

Finn was impressed with Natalia's knowledge and business acumen. Had Tristan asked her to lead this meeting because he saw her as his future liaison? If so, he wasn't sure how he felt about it. He could never see her as just a business contact.

When they reached the end of the tour Natalia asked if she could show Finn a project she had developed with Franz. 'I'm hoping you can help expand the market for it,' she explained.

Curious, he agreed.

She took him to a display of chocolate bars in distinctive pink wrapping. 'It's a premium milk chocolate, studded with freeze-dried Montovian raspberries,' she said. 'Quite irresistible.'

'Princess Natalia designed the packaging—it's the Princess Bar,' said Franz.

'All profits go towards the promotion of girls' education,' she said. 'So, you see, the more we can sell around the world, the better for girls.'

Finn spoke to her in an undertone. 'You say you haven't got a career? I think the entrepreneurial talents you've applied to your fundraising proves otherwise.'

She beamed, and again he realised how happy it made him feel to see her smile.

CHAPTER EIGHT

NATALIA WASN'T SURE which she dreaded the most—the summons to her mother's office for a queenly reprimand, or the summons to her mother's private rooms in the Queen's apartment for a mother-daughter chat.

Not long after she'd returned from her lunch meeting with Finn and the Chocolate Makers' Association, she had been invited by her mother to what she'd hoped would be the second kind of meeting. As soon as she saw her mother she suspected it might evolve into one of the queenly reprimand kind.

Her Majesty, Queen Truda, patted the place next to her on a gilded and upholstered love seat. The valuable antique was placed in front of French doors that opened to a balcony and looked down to the rose garden below. The roses had finished their autumnal flush of flowers, and now just a few frostbitten blooms were hanging on to their stems.

Her mother kissed her on both cheeks. She was elegant, blonde and had had a considerable amount of subtle surgery to keep her looking ageless.

On Natalia's twenty-fifth birthday she had suggested that Natalia was at the right age to start some preventative cosmetic work, with injectables and fillers. She had hinted that her daughter might have already left it too late to arrest wrinkles.

Natalia had politely declined. Her mother had warned her that she might regret not getting started with work on her face as soon as possible, and Natalia had gritted her teeth in an effort not to give a caustic reply.

The Queen's eyes were the same colour blue as the eyes Natalia saw when she looked in the mirror. But no amount of cosmetic surgery could erase from them the underlying sadness of being married to a man who did not love her and of having lost her firstborn son and grandson.

Right now they were narrowed—as much as her mother was able to narrow her eyes because of her frequent muscle-freezing injections. Natalia had been expecting an interrogation since the reception the night before. She was not to be disappointed.

'The Australian. Finn O'Neill. Tristan's new business associate. I saw you spent quite some time alone with him last night.'

'Yes, Mother.'

'Any longer and it would have been inappropriate.'

'Yes, Mother.' She'd learned young to agree with her mother whenever possible.

'I saw the way you looked at him.'

'What do you mean?'

'He's a very good-looking young man.'

'Yes, he is.'

'Is he the man you danced with at the wedding in Sydney?'

There was no use fibbing, or even prevaricating. Her mother would have read the bodyguard's reports. 'Yes.'

'Do you want him? In your bed, I mean?'

'*What?* Mother!'

'Well?'

Again she couldn't lie. Her mother knew her too well. 'Yes.' She couldn't lie to herself any longer, either.

'You know you can't have him?'

'Why not?'

'Because he's not suitable as a husband and you're not allowed to take a lover until after you're safely married.'

Natalia gritted her teeth. '*Why* is he not suitable for a husband? Under the new law I'm not bound to marry a royal. Finn is educated, successful, wealthy,' she said. Not to mention great company and a sensational kisser.

'*Very* wealthy. And he's squeaky clean when it

comes to his finances. No criminal record either. Not so much as a parking fine.'

'So where is your objection?'

'I can't see that your marriage to someone like Finn O'Neill could work. You—*we*—live a rarefied kind of life that people not born to it might find difficult to adapt to.'

'Gemma and Tristan are perfectly happy.'

'They're the exception—and Gemma has had some teething problems. Not the least of which is giving up her life in Australia. But, without being sexist or elitist about it, it's a rare man who is going to be happy having a wife who is far superior to him in social status.'

'Of course that's being sexist and elitist, Mother,' Natalia said, unable to let the comment go. 'Surely it would depend on the individual's attitude?'

'Or a princess could renounce her title and all that goes with it.'

Natalia gasped. 'What are you saying?'

'It's an option—although not a desirable one.' Her mother took both her hands in hers. 'We *are* talking theoretically here, aren't we, my darling?'

Natalia couldn't help a heartfelt sigh. 'Yes. Purely theoretically. There's nothing between me and Finn.'

Her mother attempted to raise her perfectly arched eyebrows. 'Nothing at all?'

Natalia sighed again. 'Okay, so I kissed him at the wedding. But that's as far as it went.'

'You're sure about that?'

'Very sure.'

'You know there are good reasons for a Montovian princess remaining chaste before her marriage? I rather like the way that British Princess put it: she "kept herself tidy".'

'I know,' Natalia said.

The words had been quoted at her before. But that British Princess had been nineteen at the time. She was twenty-seven, for heaven's sake.

'The cute young Duke... You're sure you don't want to see him again?'

'"Young" being the operative word, Mother. He's sweet, but he's only just started shaving. Besides, I suspect he's in love with his seventeen-year-old sister's best friend and is waiting for her to come of age. And, before you suggest it, I have absolutely *no* interest in meeting his uncle—the hip replacement High Duke.'

'Don't call him that. He's a very charming and cultivated man. Handsome too. He thinks you're way too young for him. Besides, he's a widower and not looking for a new wife. A discreet relationship with a mature woman closer to his age would be more appropriate.'

'Mother! *You* like him!'

'And he likes me. Who knows what might happen?'

Her mother deserved some happiness—although she was bound to her father until one of them died.

'I'm happy for you,' Natalia said.

The Queen's face softened. 'Above all, Natalia, I want you to be happy in your marriage.'

'Happy with a palace-approved man, you mean,' said Natalia. 'That's never going to work for me.'

'I want to give you the best chance to make it work,' said her mother. 'There's no divorce for the royal family, as you know.'

'I know,' Natalia said.

She could recite all the rules and regulations that governed their lives. So could her mother—who was trapped in a miserable marriage. Sometimes Natalia felt she should hate her father for what he had done to her lovely mother. But he and his mistress truly loved each other, and had done since they were teenagers. They should have been allowed to marry. It was one of the reasons her father had agreed to change the law.

'I see Tristan has included you in his business meetings with the Australian. Not his wisest move. Be careful. Try not to be alone with him. Don't encourage him.'

'Mother!'

'I mean it, my darling. Even if the law says you can marry him, I don't see how it could possibly work. Your differences are too great. And you can't have him as a lover. I don't want to see you heartbroken.'

'I don't know where this talk of marriage comes from. Certainly not from me. There is nothing between me and Finn. I hardly know him.'

Her mother's grip on her hands tightened. 'You might *say* that, my darling, but I saw the way you were looking at him last night. And the way he looked at you. Nip it in the bud. That's my advice to you as your mother and your Queen.'

An hour later Natalia sat with Finn in her favourite chocolate shop and tea room in the heart of the old town. It was ornate and old-fashioned and hadn't changed at all in her lifetime.

'The three of us loved coming here as kids,' she explained to Finn, who was opposite her at a small round table.

He looked around him at the array of premium Montovian chocolates, the displays of cakes and pastries, the splendid samovar. 'My sister and I would have thought we were in heaven.'

'We did too. Our parents were strict. And our nannies followed their rules to the letter. But a visit to this place was our special treat—a reward for good behaviour.' She paused. 'I miss my brother Carl most of all when I'm here. Carl was a chocoholic before we'd ever heard the word. He was always negotiating increases in our chocolate allowance. Never just for himself, though. Always for all three of us. He was a born leader.'

'Tristan had big shoes to fill?'

'Yes. And he's filling them remarkably well. Having Gemma as support has really helped him, I think. It was such a dark time for us when we lost Carl.'

'Did you have grief counselling to help you come to terms with his loss?'

'You sound like a counsellor yourself when you say that.'

'I just wondered. Sudden change… Unresolved grief… All could contribute to your unhappiness.' His gaze on her face was intense. 'I don't like seeing you unhappy.'

Just sitting here with him, close enough so she could reach over and touch him, was making her feel happier than she'd felt for a long time—three months, to be precise. 'I'm not as unhappy as I was.'

'Why is that?'

'Who could be unhappy sipping the best hot chocolate in the world?' *With you.*

On her trip to Australia she'd found what was

missing in her life. A relationship with a man who excited her. *Finn.*

'Good point,' he said.

'Nip it in the bud,' her mother had commanded.

Natalia had no intention of doing any such thing. She had never met a man like Finn and she intended to spend as much time as she could with him. If there was a chance to be alone with him, she would grab it. If there was a chance for her to go through with her original plan to lose her virginity to him, she would. She had a plan.

Of course it remained to be seen if Finn wanted to be any part of it.

She looked down at her watch. 'I've got my tour guide hat on again. The sun sets by five, and I would like to show you around the old town and through the cathedral while it is still light. I don't want to rush you, though. The town is beautiful, and you'll want to be able to divert down a cobbled lane or into a market square if something interests you. Our clock tower dates back to the sixteenth century. When the clock strikes the hour, medieval figures appear in rotation to strike the bell. It's quite a tourist attraction.'

'Another one of your favourite things about your home?'

'It never fails to fascinate me.'

'I look forward to seeing it. We Australians are

interested in old buildings because we don't have many of our own.'

'So that timing suits you?'

'Yes.'

'Then this evening you will dine in Tristan and Gemma's private apartment at the palace. It will be much less formal than the soirée last night. And it goes without saying that any food Gemma serves will be superlative.'

'Will you be there too?'

'Of course.'

Finn leaned over the table to be closer to her, so their heads nearly touched. He lowered his voice to barely above a whisper as there were curious onlookers at other tables in the tea room. 'Will there be a chance for us to spend time alone together?'

'Is that what you want?' She also kept her voice to a whisper.

'You bet I do.' Her heart leapt. 'What about you?'

'Oh, yes,' she said, perhaps too fervently. 'But I will have to work around a directive from the Queen that I must avoid being alone with you.'

He frowned. 'Why is that? Does she think I can't be trusted with you?'

'I believe she thinks it is me who can't be trusted with you.'

'What the hell—?' he said, forgetting to keep

his voice down. 'I mean, what the hell…?' he whispered.

She laughed.

'Laugh number three,' he said.

'What do you mean by that?' she asked, puzzled.

'I'll explain later,' he said.

She drew back from the intimacy of their heads nearly touching, made a show of pulling out her phone and scrolling through it, then spoke in a normal tone of voice.

'Tomorrow, according to your timetable, Tristan has you scheduled for morning meetings in our administrative capital of St Pierre. Tristan will accompany you for those. On your return to the palace you will be placed once more in my hands.'

Finn gave a discreet, suggestive waggling of his eyebrows, with just a hint of a leer that made her smile. 'I like that idea very much,' he said.

'Me too,' she murmured, trying not to think about what she would like to do to him with her hands. 'There's a visit to an artisan cheese producer. Then I'd like to take you out of town to visit our family's mountain chalet. It's our ski chalet in winter, but we often don't get good falls until January. A visit at this time of year will give you a taste of traditional Montovian rural life and an opportunity to hike. If we're lucky, there might be a dusting of snow.'

'I like that idea very much,' he said. 'But how—?'

She leaned over the table again. 'I'm working on how we can spend time alone. Trust me.'

'Can I really trust you?' he whispered with a wicked grin.

'Oh, yes,' she said.

At that moment the middle-aged woman Natalia had been expecting arrived and headed towards their table. Finn immediately got up from his chair.

She greeted her guest briefly in Montovian and then switched to English for introductions. 'Finn O'Neill—Anneke Blair.'

They shook hands.

'Anneke, Finn is here from Australia on a brief business trip and I've been charged with showing him around.'

Finn gestured around the tea room. 'Natalia has brought me here to chocolate heaven. What an excellent idea.'

'It is indeed,' Anneke said with a big smile.

'Anneke is married to Henry, who is originally from Surrey in the UK. He has been my English tutor since I started to speak. Anneke also speaks excellent English, and she knows more about the old town, its stories and secrets than even I do. So she will be joining us for our tour.'

'Thank you, Anneke,' Finn said. 'I appreciate you taking the time to do so.'

Her mother could have no complaints about her inclusion of Anneke. It would divert the Queen's focus from her and Finn, and it would send her the message that Natalia was, once again, being the dutiful royal daughter.

But not for long. She had plans for the chalet. *Plans for Finn.*

CHAPTER NINE

SEATED AT TRISTAN'S very hospitable dining table that evening, Finn was able to relax for the first time since he'd arrived in Montovia. The reason? He and Natalia were the only guests. And, as Gemma and Tristan were in the know about Natalia's visit to Sydney for Eliza's wedding, that meant he didn't have to hide the fact that he had met her before his visit to the palace.

Of course the extent of the time he and Natalia had spent together was still a secret shared only between them. As far as the others were concerned Natalia had danced with Finn and some of the other guests before waving the bride and groom off on their honeymoon when the wedding had wound up. Then Natalia and Finn had gone their separate ways.

That they had done nothing of the sort was a deliciously private secret between them that bubbled under their conversation and heightened the awareness between them with every glance.

Natalia sat across the table from him. She looked regally beautiful in a deep ruby-coloured velvet dress with long, tight sleeves. Adorning the creamy skin revealed by the V-neckline was an antique pendant of pearls, diamonds and rubies—no doubt a priceless family heirloom. Her hair swung loose, one side fastened over her ear with a pearl-covered hairpin.

She looked every inch the Princess, but warm and approachable too. Was it his imagination or did she look a little happier since he'd been able to make her laugh? He'd now lost count of the number of times he'd enjoyed the sound of her laughter.

To call the Crown Prince's private quarters an 'apartment' was clearly an understatement. Over two levels, it was more like a mansion. However, in contrast to the other parts of the palace Finn had seen, the design was sleek and contemporary. Natalia had whispered to him that Tristan had had the apartment gutted and redesigned after he'd inherited the Crown Prince title from Carl, to eliminate sad memories of his beloved older brother's tenure.

Wherever Finn was in the palace he was aware of the immense wealth of this royal family. Even the guest suite where he was staying was luxurious. But tonight's dinner reminded him of an evening with friends at home. Gemma had even cooked most of the meal, although there was a maid to serve and clear up.

And Gemma was obviously delighting in having a fellow Australian to chat to. 'Did you really not recognise Natalia at the soirée last night?' she asked, looking from him to her sister-in-law.

'I honestly didn't,' said Finn. 'It came as a complete surprise to me that the girl who sat next to me at the wedding was a princess in disguise.'

It was good to be able to discuss, even superficially, what he'd bottled up for three months. The way Natalia had stood him up in Sydney had been too devastating for him to share with anyone.

'I thought she looked gorgeous as a blonde,' Gemma said. 'I reckon long blonde hair is your look, Nat.'

'Thank you, Gemma,' said Natalia, smiling. She and Gemma were clearly good friends. 'But it was way too much upkeep. I'm happy to be back to my natural colouring.'

'I like it too,' said Finn, careful to keep the compliment discreet and respectful. She would look beautiful whichever way she did her hair.

'What would you have done if you'd *known* she was a secret princess?' Gemma asked.

'Probably not have dared to speak to her, let alone asked her to dance,' he said.

'And that would have been a shame,' Natalia said lightly.

'Natalia tells me your business meetings have gone well?' Tristan said.

'Very well,' said Finn. 'And I enjoyed my tours of the castle and the old town.'

'Thank you, Finn,' Natalia said, doing a good job of appearing not to show any personal interest in him. 'Tristan, that brings us to our schedule for tomorrow. After Finn's visit to St Pierre with you, we have a visit to our favourite artisan cheese producer scheduled. As it's on the way to the chalet, I plan to take Finn up to the chalet afterwards. That area is a great showcase for rural Montovia without us having to go further afield.'

'You might be cutting it fine in terms of daylight,' Tristan warned.

'You're right. And if it snows those roads could be dangerous at night... I wonder if we should plan to stay there overnight? I've invited Marco and Amelie for dinner and they're keen to stay over. Would you and Gemma like to come too?'

'I'm afraid I can't,' said Gemma. 'Shame... I love the chalet. However, I have other plans for tomorrow.'

'So do I,' said Tristan. 'But it sounds like a good idea. It's like the land that time forgot up there.'

The whole place had that air about it, Finn thought. Though he was discovering that—palaces, medieval castles and quaint towns aside—Montovia was a forward, prosperous country, and highly successful as a financial centre.

'I'll inform the housekeeper at the chalet you'll be having guests for dinner and breakfast,' said Gemma.

'That's settled, then,' said Natalia, in a very businesslike tone.

Finn didn't dare catch her eye. Clever princess. He had no doubt she'd concocted the visit to the chalet to give them some time alone together, without flagging up the fact that there might have been more to the way they'd met in Sydney.

'Well planned,' he whispered to her when he got the chance.

'Even better than swapping place cards,' she whispered back, straight faced.

The dinner had started early and ended early, as Gemma was tired. Natalia, taking her place as hostess, escorted Finn back to his room on the floor below. She didn't have to—he knew the way—but he welcomed the extra few minutes with her.

Perhaps there were security cameras about, or simply observant eyes, but she acted purely within the boundaries of her role. Until she leaned forward for just a second as she shook his hand goodnight and whispered, 'I can't wait until tomorrow.'

Finn didn't know where this thing between them could possibly go. But he was only in Montovia for another two days and he was going to grab any time he could with her without worrying about what might come next.

CHAPTER TEN

NATALIA'S ACQUAINTANCESHIP WITH full-blown insomnia had been well and truly renewed. Last night she'd hardly slept. Thoughts of Finn had relentlessly churned around and around in her mind, keeping her eyes wide open until way into the early hours.

Her obsession with Finn was almost adolescent—what was a twenty-seven-year-old woman doing, getting in such a tizz about a man she'd only known in total for a few days? For all that wedding guest psychic's predictions, and for all her mother the Queen's warnings, not a word about anything serious had passed between her and Finn.

But to her it was a very big deal.

She had never felt like this about any man. She doubted she would ever feel it again.

The disaster of their parting in Sydney had been forgiven, if not forgotten. She needed to see if Finn saw the possibility of any kind of relationship blooming between them. This sneakily planned visit to the chalet might be the only chance she got.

He returned from his meetings in St Pierre at the agreed time. Natalia had been counting the moments until she saw him again—conscious of how limited they were. They met at the top of the circular palace driveway, which led to the road that twisted its way from the castle down the mountain to the town.

Finn had changed from his business suit and was appropriately rugged up in black jeans, a grey cashmere sweater and a smart charcoal quilted coat. He was as sophisticated and stylish as any prince or duke, and a heck of a lot more handsome. Just looking at him sent shivers of want through her. But she forced herself to be professional and impartial—as if she were simply dealing with a business contact.

'A four-by-four and a uniformed chauffeur,' he said. 'Interesting choice of transport.'

'The roads can be rough around the chalet. Ice and possible snow can make them dangerous,' she said.

'Not quite what I expected for a princess-mobile.'

'The glass carriage and white horses won't cut it for today, I'm afraid,' she said, with a regretful shake of her head.

'I'm disappointed,' he said, with the grin that had the magic power to lift her spirits.

'But a princess doesn't drive herself around town,' she said. And then added as a murmured aside, 'And this way I get to sit in the back seat with you.'

Her heart was racing—not only at the thought of being alone with Finn but also at the audacity of her plan.

Being accompanied at the chalet by her cousin and his wife—both close friends who wanted to see her happy—might not be quite what her mother had in mind. But she'd had a lifetime of obedience. Her time in Sydney had made her see life with different eyes. Made her realise you had to grab opportunities when they were offered to you. You weren't always given a second chance. She fully intended to seize this one.

'Tell me about the chalet,' said Finn as he slid in next to her in the back seat. Close, but not too close.

He knew what was expected of him in public. But in private…? She shivered in anticipation.

'The chalet has nothing but happy memories for me. It's high up on the mountain, above the snow line. The building started life as a farm-house about three hundred and fifty years ago. It must have been a long way from civilisation then. In the old days the farmers were cut off from the town for most of the winter. Those remaining still live a traditional life.'

'I was beginning to think everything was ancient in your country until I saw St Pierre today. That's a very modern city.'

'Our country has one foot planted in the past

and the other striding towards the future. I'm very proud of it.'

'And the chalet now?'

'My grandfather had it converted to make a private residence. It's rustic, traditional, built from stone and timber, with sloping roofs because of the snow. Humble in its own way. But the bathrooms are new and the heating has just been updated.'

'I wouldn't expect anything less from one of *your* family residences,' he said.

'Be warned—it's no palace. My grandfather used it as a hunting lodge and it still has that kind of décor.'

'I don't hunt,' he said.

'Neither do we. We only shoot animals with a camera. The land around the chalet is a conservation area now. Some of the animals that were hunted to the point of extinction are coming back. My brothers and I were able to run wild there like we were never able to at the palace—well, our version of running wild.'

'Do you use it for skiing?'

'The chalet is not near any commercial skiing areas. But we use it as a base for cross-country skiing. The trails are wonderful. Do you ski?'

'I like skiing. But I prefer sailing.'

'Er…of course,' she said.

Natalie hoped he wasn't remembering how

she'd stood him up for their sailing date in Sydney. Then she wondered if he was a mind reader.

'Just a reminder—you don't need to say sorry again,' he said.

Compassionate. That was the word for the expression in his eyes. He now seemed to understand the challenges that came with the expectations of her privileged way of life, not just dismiss her as a 'poor little rich girl'.

She ached to reach over and take his hand. She knew it would not be wise, and yet some new rebelliousness wanted to draw his head down to hers for a kiss and do what any ordinary girl had every right to do but a princess of Montovia did not.

Instead, she shifted just a little farther away from him and forced herself to stick to the more sensible plan she had already put in place. Though his nearness, his scent, his warmth meant she was in a constant state of yearning for him.

What if he didn't feel anywhere near the same for her?

They had left behind the old town and the newer suburbs on its edge, flown through the cobblestoned villages, and were now steadily climbing the twisting roads up the mountain.

'Everywhere I look is a postcard,' said Finn. 'The land's still so green, with the colour from the trees holding the last of the autumn leaves, the black and white cows. Then there are the rustic houses and the stacks of chopped wood underneath, ready for the winter, the pumpkins piled in baskets. It's like it's all been posed for the camera.'

'Even the three tractors trundling down the middle of the road that we've had to overtake?'

'Even those,' he said with a smile. 'They were actually very smart tractors. Everything is so different from Australia—like a different world.'

'You must have seen a lot of the world for your business?'

'Yes—although I travelled first with my parents and grandparents, to visit family. Hong Kong, then Italy, Ireland later. I had a stake in all those countries—I belonged by blood. But even with our diverse background and urge to travel, we're an Australian family, through and through. Australia was good to my family. It will always be my country.'

'You're as patriotic as I am.' Somehow she hadn't thought of that. Hadn't factored in his own love of his country in her wild dreams about what might be.

'In my own way—as a citizen. As a ruler, you have a quite different relationship with your country. One I'm trying to get my head around. But I understand your connection to your family, because family is very important to me too.'

'Could you see yourself living anywhere other than Australia?' She held her breath for his answer.

'It's where I need to be. My business is based there…the Asian markets are the future for trade. I want to be part of that future.'

Natalia let out her breath on a slow sigh. 'I see.'

He turned to her. 'I had to give all that some thought when I was still at university.'

'What do you mean?'

'In my second year I spent my winter vacation in Italy.'

'Where it must have been summer?'

'Yes. I stayed in the town near Naples where my grandmother's family came from. I worked in a pizzeria, practised my Italian and met a girl. Her name was Chiara. I fell head over heels for her and she for me. I quit the pizzeria so I could spend all my time with her. Then I had to go back to Australia for uni.'

Natalia hated to think of him with another woman. It actually made her feel nauseous. She had to force her voice to sound light and neutral. 'A holiday romance?'

'It was more than that. We were engaged to be married. I thought it was for ever. I really tried to make that long-distance romance work. Once I even flew to Italy for a long weekend, so I could be with Chiara for her birthday.'

'I don't see a happy-ever-after ending to this story…' With a great effort of will, Natalia had managed to keep her voice at an even, conversational tone.

By contrast, Finn's tone darkened. 'Of course it ended. Now I can see it was inevitable. Then I was gutted. She didn't want to leave her family and friends. I had to finish my degree in Sydney. We were too young. Long story short: she met an Italian guy. She ended it with me quite brutally.'

'I'm sorry, Finn,' Natalia said—not sorry at all that he didn't get the girl, but sorry that the experience might have made him wary of long-distance relationships. 'What happened next?'

'From then on I've only dated women who live in Sydney,' he said, looking out of the window instead of at her. 'And I hold a very cynical view of love at first sight. I don't trust that it can work.'

So a girlfriend in Montovia was out of the question. Was that what he was trying to tell her? As for the 'love at first sight' comment—she wasn't sure what he meant by that either.

She decided not to try and second-guess him. Thankfully she could change the subject, as they had reached the small artisan cheesemaker who made some of the most prized cheeses in Montovia.

* * *

The cheesemaker's premises looked like yet another postcard view, Finn thought. The old stone buildings, the incredible green pastures, the mountains in the background—all were breathtakingly picturesque. Natalia brought a flash of colour in a red coat and a soft pink beret and scarf that suited her brilliantly. He liked seeing her in pink and red again rather than tones of grey.

'Before we go in, tell me again why we're here?' he asked Natalia.

'Matteo, the cheesemaker, prides himself on the quality of his handmade, cave-aged product,' she said. 'His family had always made cheeses here, but on a very small scale for local consumption. The cheese became something of a legend in Montovia and highly prized. There's a saying that good cheese makes milk immortal, and that truly applies here. Since Matteo took over he has grown the business, but still kept it on a small scale. His cheese commands top prices. He maintains exclusivity and that is one reason he doesn't want to export.'

'If he doesn't want to export, why am I seeing him?'

'For your interest,' she said. 'And so that if he ever changes his mind, he will remember you.'

'I follow your way of thinking,' he said, once

again appreciating her and Tristan's business acumen.

He also appreciated the fact that the work Tristan did with the export of his country's products was not for personal gain, but rather the promotion of Montovia.

'Although we do get a return in the form of taxes from successful businesses,' Natalia had shrewdly pointed out when he'd mentioned it.

Finn clicked immediately with Matteo—especially after they realised that while Finn's Montovian was non-existent, and Matteo's English basic, they both spoke fluent Italian, as did Natalia. He appreciated yet another side of Natalia as she spoke fluently in the language of his grandmother, complete with requisite hand gestures.

She would fit in with his family.

He shook his head to clear the thought. It was such an unlikely scenario.

Matteo took them through the process of making his cheeses. It started with milk from happy, stress-free cows, feeding on rich alpine pastures that included regional wildflowers, and ended in cool subterranean cellars, their walls lined with ancient wooden shelving stacked with wheels of prized cheese in various stages of ageing.

Finn was fascinated by it. The cheesemaking

he'd seen before had been on a much larger commercial scale. Here, tradition dictated every step. What was it Tristan had said about the land that time forgot? And Natalia was a part of that tradition, bound by customs that hardly seemed relevant to modern life. Yet like this cheese, prized for its tradition, her traditions had shaped the woman she was.

After farewells had been made, Finn headed with Natalia back to the four-by-four, carrying a wheel of Matteo's finest cheese to take to the chalet.

'I actually understand why Matteo doesn't want to lose the essence of his cheese by over-expanding, even though I would very much like to have his business,' he said.

'I liked seeing your passion for the cheese,' she said. 'I understand now why you're so successful in your business—you care.'

Finn saw immediately why Natalia loved the Montovian royal family's chalet. It might have started off as a humble, rustic farmhouse, but it was now every bit the luxurious mountain retreat, in a traditional style of carved timber and stone, leather and wool.

Finn was wealthy, and he came from a comfortably off family, but the extent of privilege enjoyed by the royal family was staggering. The chalet kept a year-round staff, whose brief was to have the place ready at any time for the family to use—which seemed wildly extravagant. Although at the same time, it kept practically a cavalry of staff in employment.

He needed to keep his mind open—not view Natalia's life burdened with his preconceived ideas of what a princess should be.

Natalia introduced Finn to the middle-aged grey-haired housekeeper Hanna, and her husband the caretaker, Bernard. Finn was surprised when she greeted them with warm hugs and rapid chattering in Montovian. The caretakers did not speak English.

'Hanna was one of our nannies when I was young,' Natalia explained when they were on their own, coats off, enjoying a hot drink.

She looked elegant again, in slim trousers and a cream cashmere turtle neck. The room was heated by a blazing log fire in the most enormous carved stone fireplace Finn had ever seen.

'Hanna was loyal to us, and we are loyal to her. She is considered to be—what's the English phrase?—a family retainer.'

Natalia's English was so fluent Finn was surprised at the occasional reminder that it was not her native tongue.

'Hanna seems a nice person,' he said.

'She's warm and kind. Often we were left here

with just Hanna and Bernard to look after us. We trust them both implicitly.'

'I've been meaning to ask… No bodyguards for you in Montovia? Or have I just not noticed them?'

'The royal family is loved here. We feel safe in our own homes, our own country. Common-sense precautions are taken, of course—particularly in crowds.' She looked up at him, a smile dancing on her lips. 'By the way, there are no security cameras here.'

Finn liked the emphasis she'd put on the absence of surveillance. He could hardly wait to have her to himself, even if only for a few minutes, with no thought of anyone observing them together. If things went his way, they would need their privacy…

Natalia had placed him in a comfortable guest room at the other end of the chalet from her room. Her cousin and his wife would stay in the room adjoining hers. Finn wished his room was closer to Natalia's. However, no doubt room placement had to follow protocols like everything else.

'I'm near my cousin and Amelie,' she'd explained. 'But you'll find them sympathetic to our need to spend some time together while never appearing to be on our own.'

'Why is that?' He had met Marco and Amelie

at the soirée on his first evening, and had enjoyed their company.

'Until the law was changed they were unable to marry because Amelie was a commoner. They had to keep their relationship secret. I sometimes manoeuvred things so they could be together.'

'So they want to return the favour?' he said approvingly.

Much as he liked the Count and his doctor wife, the Countess, he still wished he had Natalia all to himself. His imagination played with the idea of kissing her, of peeling off her clothes on that densely fluffy rug in front of the log fire, seeing the flickering shadows from the flames playing on her creamy skin.

But then it seemed the staff would always be present, so that was a scenario that was unlikely ever to be played out.

Marco and Amelie arrived, greetings were exchanged, and it was decided that the four of them would go for a hike on the trails through the forest surrounding the house.

'The light is already starting to fade,' Natalia said. 'So we won't go too far from the chalet.'

Finn was eager to get outside after their time cooped up in the car, luxurious as it was. He also wanted to snatch any opportunity to be alone with Natalia. He was only too conscious of the hours ticking away towards the time for his departure

from Montovia the following afternoon. There were things to be said, decisions to be made. Non-verbal communication too, of the more intimate kind.

The chalet was not far behind them when Marco said he thought he'd spotted red deer and wanted to peel off from the pathway. Amelie followed him. Not a word was spoken but the message was clear. They were getting away to give them space.

He was alone with Natalia. At last.

CHAPTER ELEVEN

AT LAST. FOR three long months Natalia had dreamed of being in Finn's arms again. Now they were alone. She was trembling with awareness and anticipation. There was every chance it might happen.

It *had* to happen. She would die if it didn't. Not literally—she had never had suicidal thoughts. But her soul had shrivelled that morning she had left Finn behind in Sydney. And in the following months she knew her family had been worried about her mental health.

She'd been worried about her mental health. So much so that she'd sought medical advice. She'd been unable to be completely honest, though— rather she had explained that she'd broken up with an unsuitable man and was unable to come to terms with it.

The doctor had diagnosed situational depression, caused by a traumatic event in her life, and Natalia had done her best to follow the advice given on how to alleviate her symptoms. But it hadn't been until she'd seen Finn again that the cloud had started to lift.

Her life was fulfilling in so many ways. It wasn't that she needed a man to take it to another level. She needed *Finn*. She hadn't known what was missing until she'd met him, lost him and then been fortunate enough to have him fall back into her life. Now she'd been given a second chance to be with him, to get to know him, to discover if what she thought she felt about him was real.

Worth breaking the rules real.

Now she stood facing him under the canopy of a thicket of spruce trees against a chilly blue sky. The forest seemed still and silent with expectation.

'Have they gone?' Finn asked.

Natalia nodded, too choked to utter a word. She looked up at him, thrilled by the intensity of his expression, his green eyes focused solely on her.

'Good,' he said.

He pulled her into his arms.

At last. Her heart sang.

She was wearing gloves, and so was he, but even through the layers of both their padded jackets she could feel his strength, his warmth.

Finn. She sighed her joy and relief. This was where she wanted to be. It had been three very long months since their last kiss. She couldn't wait a second longer for another.

She wound her arms around his neck and pressed her mouth to his, closed her eyes at the bliss of it, the tenderness, the way he tasted of coffee with a hint of toothpaste. He'd been expecting to kiss her. Maybe wanting it as much as she did.

'Finn…' she murmured urgently against his lips.

He kissed her back, his mouth firm and warm on hers, and there were no further words.

The kiss grew deeper, more demanding, more *thrilling*. Their breathing became more ragged, loud in the still of the forest. Her knees threatened to sag beneath her. Holding her tight, he nudged her towards a tree so her back rested against it. That made it easier for him to unbutton her jacket, to pull off his gloves and drop them on the forest floor, to slide his hands, bare and warm, under her jacket.

She gasped as he tugged her sweater from the waistband of her trousers, slid his hands around her waist. His hands felt so good on her bare skin. Three months of banked-up desire ignited and flared until she burned for him—more touch, more kisses, *more Finn*.

'You're wearing rather more clothes than when I last kissed you,' he said, his voice deep and husky.

Last time she'd been wearing just a pink lacy bra and tiny lacy panties. She flushed at the memory of it. She was wearing the same now—though in a smaller size.

'You're more encumbered too,' she murmured,

as she stripped off her gloves and fumbled with the belt of his jacket, annoyed with herself that she wasn't more adept.

He pulled back from the kiss, panting. 'Any chance we can continue where we left off in Sydney?'

'Yes, please,' she said, scarcely able to get the words out. 'Though it's a tad chilly to get naked out here.'

But if he wanted to make love to her in the forest, if he wanted to lay her down on a bed of pine needles, she'd still say yes. Which was all kinds of crazy. And exciting. And likely to lead to frostbite in uncomfortable places.

'Are there bears and wolves?' he asked.

'Maybe,' she said. 'More likely foxes. And rabbits. Hares, too.'

'Hmm…' he said, nuzzling her neck. 'The rabbits don't scare me.'

'The hares can get a bit scary when they fight.'

'Maybe out here isn't the best place,' he said, releasing her with obvious reluctance. 'And not just because of the dangerous hares.'

'Wise decision,' she said, though her words were tinged with regret.

What if they didn't get another chance?

Her hair had got tousled and he smoothed an errant lock away from her forehead in a gesture that sent pleasure shimmying through her.

'Getting together isn't so easy this time, is it?' he said hoarsely. 'Back then we were two regular people, struck by an instant attraction, and possibilities were opening up ahead of us. We could choose what we wanted to do about them. It seemed so uncomplicated. Now we know how very complicated our situation is.'

'I know only too well,' she said.

'Try not to be alone with him.' Her mother's words hadn't been in the slightest bit ambiguous. *Sorry, Mother.*

He cupped her face in his large warm hands, looked deep into her eyes with an intensity that thrilled her as much as a caress.

'I still want you, Natalia. More than anything, I want you.'

'I want you too, Finn. I never stopped wanting you.'

'Back then I knew nothing about you except that I wanted you. Now I know everything I need to know.'

She stilled. 'Not quite everything,' she said, in a very small voice.

'What do you mean?' His face tightened and his hands dropped from around her to his sides. 'More secrets? More lies?'

She could see the disappointment in the twist of his mouth, hear it in in his voice.

'Nothing like that,' she said.

'No more big surprises—please, Natalia. Finding out you were a completely different person
was surprise enough for me. I don't know that I
can deal with any more.'

'It's not that. I have no more identities. No more
lies. It's just…'

'What?' he said.

'Do you remember that night? In my hotel
room?'

He grinned—a slow, sexy grin that sent a shud-
der of want spiralling through her.

'As if I'd ever forget.'

'Back then I told you I hadn't done that kind
of thing before…'

'I remember. I guessed you weren't in the habit
of taking a man you didn't know very well back
to your hotel room. But it felt like we'd known
each other for a long time, didn't it? That we knew
each other well enough to—'

'You're right. I had never taken a man back to
my room. But you have to understand I—'

'Hell, Nat, you don't think I'd pass judgement
on you for that? I'm not in the habit of hop-
ping into bed with someone I scarcely know,
either. It was special that night. We both wanted
each other too much to wait. We both knew the
score.'

She bent down to pick up her gloves from
where she'd tossed them on the ground. Pulled

them slowly back on, first her right hand, then her left. *Delaying tactics.*

'That's just it. I didn't know the score. I didn't know *anything.*'

He frowned. 'I'm not sure what you're getting at.'

She looked down at the ground. Noticed his gloves were there too. She should pick them up for him. They were good ones. Leather lined with cashmere.

'When I said I hadn't done it before, I meant *any* of it. I... I hadn't done more than kissing.' Finally she looked up at him. 'I... I'm a virgin, Finn. A twenty-seven-year-old virgin.'

He stared at her, incredulous. If it hadn't been so serious she would have laughed out loud at the expression on his face.

'You're not serious? You seemed...experienced.'

She screwed up her face. 'I was learning as I went along. I'd never undone a man's shirt before in my life. You were a brilliant tutor.'

'I wouldn't have known. I couldn't tell. There was no need for tutoring. But why?'

'A Montovian princess is meant to go to her marriage a virgin. It's tradition. Certainty that the husband's heirs are his own is the theory. I should have been married by the time I was twenty. But, as you know, I resisted that idea and I got older and older. I've been waiting longer than was anticipated.'

'Whoa… This is taking some getting used to.' He ran his hand through his hair so it stood up in spikes.

'You don't mind?'

'Of course I don't mind. Why would I mind?'

'It's odd, I know.'

'There's nothing odd about it. It's just unbelievable. Although quite precious in a way. You've really never made love with a man?'

'Not even come close.'

'Surely you've fooled around?'

'No. You've got to understand, I've never met anyone I wanted to fool around with. There was a boy at uni I liked. But as soon as my parents got wind that I was seeing him they paid him off and I never saw him again. Remember, I've always been destined for a marriage with someone of suitable rank. Fooling around just wouldn't do. Besides, me being a princess was a barrier. Before you, there was someone who interested me—but it never went anywhere because he didn't want the spotlight that he knew would be on him if we dated. All I met were those suitable suitors.'

'Who were entirely *un*suitable?'

'You were the first man to see me in my underwear.'

He groaned. She was fascinated by the depth of agony in his groan.

'Don't remind me of how sensational you looked. Pink lace against creamy skin...your beautiful long legs. How have you endured going without sex?'

'It's never seemed a hardship until now. I didn't feel I was missing out. I'd never met a man I wanted. Until...until you.'

She looked up at him. Her heart jolted at how utterly handsome he was. She still could hardly believe her hot guy from the wedding was here.

'You seemed so willing.'

'I *was* willing. Believe me, I was willing. I intended to lose my virginity to you.'

'You *what*? That night? It was to be your first time?'

'It might sound cheesy, but you woke me up.' She felt suddenly shy, but this needed to be said. 'The first time you kissed me you turned on a switch that flooded me with wants and needs I'd never felt before. It was time.'

'You chose *me*?'

'I chose you.'

He turned away from her, as if to gather his thoughts. Then he swung back to face her. 'I wish you'd told me. It's quite a responsibility for a man to be a woman's first lover. To make sure she enjoys herself.'

'Oh, I knew I was going to enjoy myself. The way you touched me, the way you made me feel…' Her heart raced at the memory of it.

He groaned again. 'Natalia, no. Don't remind me. Not out here, where we can do nothing about it.'

'Sorry,' she said, not feeling sorry at all, and loving the power she had to arouse him as he aroused her.

'But you stopped me. I thought that you'd suddenly realised how impetuous you were being. We were moving too fast.'

She sighed. How many times since had she regretted stopping him?

'The protection thing pulled me back to reality. All that stuff I'd blocked because I wanted more than anything for you to carry me to that bed and make love to me. It brought home to me the seriousness of what I intended to do—the risks I would be taking. But most of all I knew I was going back home in the morning. It was so new to me—to want a man the way I wanted you. To make love with you just the once and never again would have been devastating. It wasn't just about the rules. I was protecting my emotions too.'

He frowned. 'Why didn't you tell me at the time that you're a virgin?'

She took a deep breath. This topic took her sailing back into the troubled waters of her deception. 'Because then I would have had to tell you the truth about who I really was. And I just couldn't. Not then, and not afterwards.'

'And now?'

'Nothing has changed as far as my royal obligations go. But you've come back into my life and I want you just as much. More so.'

'What does that mean for us?' he said.

'You...you're saying there's an "us"?'

He turned. 'Come on, let's walk further into the forest. I need to think.'

'Good idea.'

She stooped, picked up his gloves, caught up with him, handed them to him. He stared at them for a moment, as if he didn't know what they were, before shoving them in his jacket pocket. She realised how difficult, how inconceivable, this—her life, the only life she had known—must seem to him.

He held out his hand to her and she took it. She walked alongside him, steering him in a different direction from the one she knew her cousin and his wife had taken.

He spoke again. 'At the wedding I started to wonder about an *us*—an impossible "us". Because you—so I thought—lived in England, and I'd tried long-distance before and it had been a disaster.'

'I can see that,' she murmured. She thrilled

to his words. So he'd felt it too, back at the wedding—not just physical attraction, something more, something real, something life-changing.

'But still I started to think of ways I could perhaps *make* it work. Then… You know what happened next. You disappeared. An *us* was never going to happen because there wasn't a *you*. Then, at the soirée, the impossible, the amazing, the unbelievable happened and you came into my life again—a *you* who both was and wasn't *you*—and I couldn't see that there could ever be an *us*.'

It was a long speech, but Natalia had listened, enthralled. 'And now?'

'All I can think of is how much I want there to be an us. How much I want *you*. When we were admiring those vats of chocolate at the Montovian chocolate factory I was thinking about you, and how wonderful it was to be sharing the experience with you. When I was sampling Matteo's cheeses I was thinking about how much I wanted to have my arm around you.'

'And you are in my thoughts constantly. That you're actually here in Montovia makes me want to dance down the street.'

'The entire way up here in the car, admiring the scenery, all I wanted to do was pull you into my arms and kiss you senseless.'

'Why didn't you?' she asked, breathless.

'Because this is so much more complicated

than us simply living in different countries on other sides of the world. You're the Princess of Montovia and I'm an Aussie guy from Sydney. The obstacles are onerous. Not just because you're a princess. Not just because you live on the other side of the world from me. But because when it comes to my personal life, I'm a cautious kind of guy. I don't let myself get involved too easily. Dip my toe in the water before I dive right in. I've steered clear of serious relationships while I've been building the business so rapidly. I don't need the distraction of anyone making demands on me.'

'Oh,' she said. The hot guy she remembered from the wedding had seemed anything but cautious.

'But when I met you at the wedding caution didn't get a look-in. I wanted to jump straight in without hesitation. And was so glad I did because you were amazing. Then I thought I'd never see you again. Now here you are. What a rollercoaster. Man, am I distracted. I *want* to be distracted. But all we had was a few hours in Sydney with no time to develop anything more than initial sparks. Is that enough to be an *us*?'

'It's a start. And what's wrong with a strong start?'

He stopped. Turned to her. Put his hands on her shoulders. Urgently searched her face.

'We need to talk. Because if there is a way ahead for us, now is the time for us to set our feet on the path. If there isn't, then we have to walk away before we really hurt each other and—'

The sound of stamping feet and muffled laughter, of loud rustlings in the undergrowth made them jump apart.

'Marco and Amelie—warning us of their approach,' she said.

She brushed her hair away from her face. 'Quickly. Do I look okay? Will they be able to tell we've been kissing?'

He kissed her again—swiftly, fiercely. 'You look adorable, beautiful…your cheeks flushed, your eyes sparkling. I want the world to know you've just been thoroughly kissed by me. I don't want us to be skulking around bushes and hiding. We need to talk about our options.'

'We have options?' Could she allow herself to hope?

'Everyone has options. Even the impossible *us*. We need to analyse and weigh them up if we're to find our path.'

'That sounds so businesslike.'

'That's the way I am. I don't trust infatuation as a basis for life-long relationships.'

'Do you think this—between us—is just infatuation?' She didn't doubt what she felt for him went way beyond infatuation.

'I don't know. But it feels like something much deeper. It did from the get-go, if I'm to be honest. But it came from nowhere. Lasting relationships to me are partnerships based on a long getting to know each other process. We haven't been given that. It's like we're in a crucible. Your family doesn't talk dating—it talks *marriage*. Advance to "Go" before I've even got a counter on the board. I always expected there to be time for me to get to know a woman before the word marriage entered into it.'

'You make it sound impossible.' She put her hands to her face in despair.

Gently he took them away, looked into her face. 'Not impossible. Possibilities are what we have to talk about. In the meantime, I suggest you smooth down your hair, wipe that smear of lipstick from the corner of your mouth—here, I'll do it—then straighten your scarf, and by the time we get back to the chalet you'll look like all you did on this walk in the forest was explain to me about the re-generation of the wildlife and point out the eagle soaring above us in the sky.'

'What eagle?' she asked, looking above her.

When the others appeared, with Marco calling out an alert, that was what they found—her talking to an attentive Finn in her best tour guide voice.

'And that very eagle, represented with a sword

in its beak, is on the crest of the royal family of Montovia.'

Clever Finn for thinking on his feet. For making her laugh. For making her think about possibilities.

But was what they had enough? Was it just infatuation? The thrill of the forbidden? Could she trust whatever had ignited so quickly between them?

When there was a ticking clock on the amount of time they had together how did she know he could give her what she wanted? True love. The kind princesses got in fairy tales, with happy-ever-afters, but the kind that had always seemed elusive to her as a real-life princess.

CHAPTER TWELVE

USUALLY THERE WAS nothing Finn enjoyed more in cold weather than a hearty meal and a good red wine enjoyed in a room lit by a roaring fire. It was the stuff of fantasy for an Australian boy from subtropical Sydney.

Hell, this whole situation he found himself in was the stuff of fantasy.

He was falling for a princess.

But he didn't know if it was real. He didn't have anything to compare it to except that long-ago romance with Chiara, which had seemed real enough at the time, but certainly hadn't felt anything like this.

This intensity, this overwhelming longing to be with Natalia, was something powerful and compelling. He recognised it as the most important emotion he had ever felt. But it was a recognition tinged with caution. He didn't trust sudden flames that could die out as quickly as they'd flared. Those flames had not been enough to sustain a relationship with Chiara.

The strong marriages in his family were based on partnerships. Didn't that require a slow burn, a getting-to-know-each-other before any commitment was considered? He wanted certainty.

Could he get that with Natalia? He had no idea where such powerful feelings could drive him. But he knew he could not dismiss them.

He was seated next to Natalia at a long wooden table designed for way more than four, but cosy enough just the same. She wore a long purple velvet skirt and a long-sleeved scoop-neck silk knit top in silver—her version of informal dress. His black jeans and black cashmere turtleneck seemed more than appropriate.

At the table, he was being careful to keep a respectable distance apart from her, but she occasionally slipped her hand into his under cover of the tablecloth. Amazing how the simple act of holding hands could be so thrilling when it was with the woman he wanted almost beyond reason.

He didn't want to let her go.

'Did you enjoy our menu based on traditional homestyle favourites?' she asked in her best hostess voice. But her eyes showed more than a hostess should to a single male guest. Did anyone else notice?

'The cabbage pie was delicious—something new for me. And the roast was superb—I really liked the warm potato salad.'

They were talking about potatoes!

He smiled and surreptitiously squeezed her hand. This single male guest probably wasn't doing a great job of masking his feelings, either.

He suspected Marco and Amelie were aware of what was brewing between him and Natalia, and were complicit without actually coming out in the open with their approval.

The housekeeper was a different matter altogether.

'Hanna keeps glaring at me,' he murmured to Natalia. 'Do you think she's on to us?'

'No doubt she suspects something—she's fond of me and she wouldn't want to see me hurt. Her generation is fearful of any transgressions of the rules.'

'And you?'

'I need to know which rules I'm prepared to break,' she whispered. 'And the repercussions I'm prepared to suffer.'

His grip on her hand tightened.

They had to talk.

The evening passed very pleasantly, although all Finn wanted to do was speak to Natalia on her own. He was scheduled to leave Montovia after a mid-morning business meeting the next day, which she was chairing on behalf of Tristan. The clock was ticking down on the time they had together.

It turned out that Marco and Amelie were just as good companions at dinner as they had been at the soirée. Finn learned a lot about living in contemporary Montovia, where young people were testing the old, traditional ways. And they, in turn, were curious about Australia.

'I would love to visit Sydney,' Amelie said.

'You and Marco would be most welcome as my guests if you do so,' said Finn. 'I have a large house on the harbour with several guest rooms.'

'And you, Natalia—you have always wanted to see Sydney, especially after Tristan found his beloved wife there,' said Marco.

Natalia choked on her chocolate pudding but quickly recovered herself. 'Yes, it is a dream of mine. I might even find myself a husband there.'

It was Finn's turn to choke on his pudding. He quickly downed a glass of Montovian spring water, drawn from a well on the property.

Amelie frowned. 'Is there something allergenic in this pudding? Please tell me before I try it…'

'Not to my knowledge,' Natalia said in a faint voice, fanning her face with her hand. 'Just…just the sauce is a little hot.'

Finn wished he could be open and honest about how he'd met Natalia. He wasn't accustomed to lying. Sooner or later he would blunder and make some indiscreet comment that might let the cat out of the bag.

Not long after dessert Marco asked permission for himself and Amelie to leave the table and retire to their room.

'He has to ask because I'm higher in rank than

he is,' Natalia explained, after they'd said good-night to the Count and his wife.

She led Finn to the adjoining room. Three large, comfortable brown leather sofas were arranged in front of another toasty fire. Stacked firewood was shelved on both sides of the fireplace and large metal fire tools hung from a rack. The fire gave a warm, inviting glow to the room, and the only other lighting was from table lamps.

'You have to give him *permission*? Even though he's your cousin…your friend?'

'We're so used to how things work, we don't question it,' she explained. 'I'm not sure that is something Tristan would be able to convince our father to change—not quickly anyway.'

Natalia sat on the sofa facing the fireplace and patted the seat next to her.

'I don't have to ask your permission to be seated?' he said.

She laughed. 'Of course not. You're a foreigner.'

He sighed, and knew it sounded heavy with the weight of his concerns. 'No wonder I find it difficult to get a handle on how it all works.'

'I understand how difficult it is for one not born to it. Gemma found it a steep learning curve. She says she still has much to learn. Not just about being royal, but also about being Montovian. But she's very happy with Tristan and has become a remarkable Crown Princess.'

Finn took his place next to Natalia on the sofa, sitting a polite distance away from her. If someone were to come into the room unexpectedly they would see nothing untoward.

Hell, Natalia's experience with men seemed so limited he wondered if the King and Queen posted surveillance on her dates. He shifted a few inches farther away from her, just to be sure, then angled his body towards her in an entirely acceptable conversational manner.

'Talking of Gemma—what is it about her and Amelie both wanting to go to bed so early?' he said. 'Don't they ever want to party? Is that a Montovian thing?'

'I suspect it's a woman in the early stages of pregnancy thing. Didn't you see Amelie's horror at the prospect of something harmful in the pudding?'

'A mere male wouldn't notice such a thing.'

'Women are attuned to notice such things in their friends. But we also respect the fact that women usually don't want to make any announcement until the pregnancy is safely established.'

'You think Gemma might be pregnant?'

'I suspect so—though we're such good friends I'm surprised she hasn't shared the news with me. I can't help but be concerned that something might be wrong, but I suspect she's simply being cautious.'

'If she and Tristan had a baby wouldn't it kick you down the line of succession? Perhaps she's worried that might upset you?'

'Upset me? I would be glad to be demoted in such a way. It would make my life so much easier.'

Hanna entered the room and Natalie had a quick exchange in Montovian with her. Then she turned to him. 'Hanna wants to know if you would like anything further. A camomile tea, perhaps?'

Finn shook his head. 'Nothing for me, thanks.' He looked up at Hanna and thanked her in Montovian. The older woman beamed at him before she turned to leave the room.

'Finn! You spoke in Montovian. When did you learn that?'

'Don't get too excited. I asked Tristan to teach me how to say "please" and "thank you" before we went into our meetings in St Pierre. Just to be polite. I think I've mastered it.'

'Your accent was perfect. Well done.'

He was glad she was pleased. Montovian would not be an easy language to master. But, as his mother often said, the first new language was the most difficult. The more languages you learned, the easier it became.

He watched as Hanna's back view faded from

sight. As if by mutual agreement, he and Natalia both stayed very still and listened for sounds from the next room.

'When Hanna finishes in the kitchen will she go to bed too?' Finn asked.

'House servants in the royal households are obligated to be on call until the family and their guests have retired.'

'So if we stayed up all night, until sunrise, she and Bernard would have to stay up all night too?'

'That's how it works,' she said.

He frowned.

'You're aching to say something, aren't you?' she said.

'No. These are your ways and I'm not one to criticise. Where do they live?'

'Their home is a large, comfortable apartment beyond the kitchen.'

'What if we want to contact them for camomile tea?'

'There's a buzzer connected to their apartment. But I can't remember how long since it has been used. It might even need a new battery.'

'What do they do while they're waiting for the battery-less buzzer?'

'I have no idea. Perhaps watch television in bed?'

He smiled. 'And that's how you work around "how it works".'

'Tristan and I have our methods of getting around the old ways.'

'Which brings us back to us.' He looked around. 'Can we talk privately here?'

'As long as we keep our voices down.'

'I have no intention of shouting. But I *would* like to kiss you.' He kissed her on the cheek—a sweet, simple kiss. 'That's for being kind to your old nanny.'

She kissed him on the mouth. Just as quick, just as sweet. 'That's for you being you.'

He caught her hand, clasped it with his. 'Why do we have to skulk around? If I was here longer, couldn't we date? Your family want you to marry someone they consider suitable, but now there's no law against you choosing who you want to have in your life. This is such an artificial, pressure cooker situation.'

'As I told you, you're the first man I've been seriously attracted to. I guess I'm not sure how to handle it. I could scream and yell and defy my family—insist I want to be with you. Then you'd go back to Sydney, I'd never see you again and I'd have a lot of bridge-building to face with my family.'

'I want you. I like you. And I'd like to get to know you—not as a princess, with all the complications that comes with, but as a woman. Like we did at the wedding. I asked you on a date in Sydney. Have you ever wondered what might have happened if you'd spent that day with me on my yacht?'

'Many times…over three miserable months.'

'I searched for you for weeks, you know?'

'You must have been furious with me. Yet you searched for me?'

'Furious, yes—but worried, too, that you might have come to some harm. My male ego wouldn't let me accept that you could just walk away from the magic we'd shared simply because you didn't like me.'

She gasped. 'You *know* it wasn't that.'

'I know now. Back then I wanted an explanation for how you could just disappear. I thought you might have been kidnapped. Bundled into a boat. Thrown overboard from a ferry. I had all sorts of insane ideas. Anything but face up to the fact you'd played me. That for some reason you'd got me enchanted with you—got me believing you might be just a bit enchanted with me—and then callously dumped me.'

'I was actually very taken with you. That's the thing with enchantments. They entice and snare both ways.'

He kissed her again. So what if they were seen? He almost wanted them to be seen so they could be open about what was happening between them. But he suspected Natalia would suffer the consequences. Would she always be under the thumb of her parents because they were also her King and Queen?

'My next thought was it had to have been a scam. I checked my credit cards—perhaps when I'd gone to the bathroom you could have scanned them—but, no. My bank balance remained intact. My identity hadn't been stolen.'

She smiled. 'I don't exactly need the money.'

He smiled back. He'd appreciated her sense of humour from the get-go. 'Finally, when my desire to know more about you overcame my reluctance to admit my humiliation, I asked Eliza. The first person on her doorstep after she returned from her honeymoon was me, begging for details about Natalie Gerard.'

'Eliza? But she—'

'She kept your secret. She's loyal.'

'Good,' she said, with visible relief.

'I can still see my friend, standing there with her hands on her hips. *"I told you Natalie might not be who she said she was."* Her pity, and her righteous indignation that I hadn't listened to her, rubbed salt into my already stinging humiliation.'

'Poor Finn,' said Natalia.

'Poor Finn?' He snorted. 'I didn't get any information or sympathy from Eliza. *"I tried to warn you"*—that was all she said. Not one more word could I get out of her. Except yet another offer to fix me up with the world's most boring woman—Prue, whose place card we switched at the wedding.'

'Eliza called me at about that time,' Natalia said thoughtfully. 'Asked me if I remembered you. Of course I stuck to the script and said I'd danced with you at the wedding and we'd had coffee afterwards, but that was as far as it had gone. Mind you, while you were trying to find *me* I was frantically looking *you* up on the internet. Of course I found everything you'd told me about yourself was the truth. While all I had done was lie. I was a mess—couldn't eat, couldn't sleep...just torn apart by regret.'

'I had some crazy ideas about what had happened to you. But none nearly as crazy as what turned out to be the truth.'

'And yet you've forgiven me?'

'Because I've never met a woman who attracts me like you do—first as Natalie, now as Natalia. The more I know you the more attracted I am, and the more I find to admire in you.'

He was rewarded by her lovely smile, which lit up her eyes. 'I feel the same about you. I've really enjoyed our time working together.'

He leaned over to kiss her.

Natalia put up her hand to stop him. 'You know we really can't be caught kissing in here... We can't risk Bernard coming in to check if the fire needs another log, or to stoke it, or whatever one does with fires. Or Hanna coming in just wanting to keep an eye on me.'

He pulled back from her. 'Why? These constrictions seem unnecessary. We're both single. We're not hurting anyone by getting to know each other. Or kissing each other. And this fire is kinda romantic. Guy-type romantic, I mean. Forget the flowers and the girly frills. This is what does it for me. A warm rug, the flickering flames, cosy dark corners…and you and I snuggled on that rug needing nothing more than each other to warm us—'

'Stop it,' she said. 'That scenario does it for me, too. I want you Finn. It's torture sitting next to you on this sofa not being able to kiss you, touch you, explore you.'

He shifted in his seat, groaned. 'I can't believe you don't know what that kind of talk does to me.'

'I might have an idea, because I'm feeling the same way.'

She took a deep breath, which only succeeded in focusing his gaze on the swell of her curves in her snug-fitting top.

'Best then, I guess, that we're not distracted,' she said. 'No kissing…no touching.'

'But only because we've decided we don't want the distraction. Not because someone else has put strictures on us.'

'Agreed,' she said.

She turned to face him, their knees nudged and she didn't move back. Again he had the feeling that he'd fallen into a fantasy. It was as if she had conjured up this room—the blaze of the fire, the fresh smell of pine, and his beautiful dark-haired virgin Princess wrapped in her flowing long skirt like a woman in a medieval manuscript...or a movie...or a game.

He wanted the fantasy to be real.

He shifted away from the distracting contact, determined to move things along before Bernard appeared to tend to the fire, or the ancient metallic clock on the wall struck midnight and he was left on his own with only smouldering ashes, longing for one of the most unattainable women in the world.

'In my world, where we could date and get to know each other, and see if what we feel is infatuation or something deeper, I wouldn't be mentioning marriage so soon. But it seems your family want you on a fast track to marriage. No time for feelings to develop. No time for compatibility to be established. No time to be sure it's going to work.'

Her mouth turned down and her eyes clouded. 'We are a family who lost our heir—a beloved son, brother, husband, father—and his son.'

Finn wondered, not for the first time, why

both heirs had been travelling together in one helicopter.

'Perhaps, as a result, my parents have become a little obsessive about ensuring the line of succession. Their great fear is the throne going to my uncle's branch of the family—who are dissolute, to say the least. That's not Marco's father, by the way, it's a different uncle. They want my children to be in line as back-up, I suppose.'

'Even though they would come after Tristan, and after his children and then after you? It's not likely they'd ever inherit the throne.'

'Not likely—but possible.'

'But even before your brother's death, you resisted an arranged marriage?'

'I believe in love and only love as a basis for marriage. Don't you?'

'Of course I do. A love that grows based on compatibility and shared interests and proves to be real. A partnership. After a long engagement. That's how it works in my family. My grandparents and my parents are happily married. Each anniversary is a big deal to be celebrated.'

'It's the total opposite in my family. I've told you about my parents and my grandparents. But it was my brother's marriage that really made me wary. Carl was introduced to Sylvie as a potential bride. She was beautiful and vivacious and he fell for her as she seemed to fall for him. But she didn't love Carl. She loved the idea of being Crown Princess, with all the wealth and status that came with it. She was demanding and capricious and she made his life hell. Once she'd had Rudi I don't think they even shared a bed. Poor Carl was so unhappy. Seeing that, I decided I'd rather stay single than marry a nobleman I didn't love. And then Carl died.'

He had to ask. 'Why were they all travelling in the same helicopter?'

'Because Sylvie insisted she didn't want to fly with Rudi behind Carl, in what she saw as a lesser helicopter not befitting her status. And, as he did so many times, he gave in to her to avoid a tantrum.'

'I'm so sorry,' he said. 'Such a tragedy.'

He pulled her to him in a hug and she did not resist. He wanted to protect her, this woman who was usually protected by two bodyguards, to wrap her in warmth and security and take away her pain. To make her laugh every day.

'When Tristan changed the rules more choices opened to me. But my parents can still withhold permission for me to marry someone of whom they disapprove.'

He considered her statement. 'They could make your life uncomfortable if they withheld their permission?'

'*Very* uncomfortable,' she said.

'Would dungeons be involved?'

'Who knows?' She laughed. 'Seriously? Not likely at all. And, apart from needing palace-sanctioned permission, I love my parents and want them to approve of my choice of husband and father for my children. And there can be no other option for me than marriage. Living with a man would never be sanctioned.'

'No doubt I'm not high on the approved list?'

'They believe a royal marriage has a better chance of working if both husband and wife come from the same social strata.'

'Yet that didn't work for Carl,' he said. 'And Tristan chose his own wife—breaking more than one tradition in the way he did it.'

'I could, as a citizen of Montovia, marry without the King and Queen's permission. It's me as a princess who needs it.'

He groaned. 'There's another obstacle around every corner. But I don't want to walk away from you, Natalia. I felt lost without you in St Pierre today.'

'And the palace seemed empty without you while you were away. I was counting the minutes until you returned. I'll really miss you when you leave tomorrow. I wish I could stow away in your luggage.'

'I like that idea. But you live in Montovia, with

all the responsibilities entailed in your position as Princess and second in line to the throne.'

'And you live in far-away Australia, where your family is and your successful business.'

The logs in the fire shifted and moved in a shower of sparks. The huge, old-fashioned pendulum on the metallic clock on the wall tick-tocked the seconds away. Finn was conscious of their time together dwindling away.

He slowly shook his head. 'It's never going to be a simple boy-meets-girl scenario for us.'

'No. The stakes are so much higher when it's a princess and a millionaire tycoon.'

'But so are the potential gains,' he said, tracing his finger down her cheek and across the outline of her mouth so she trembled. He didn't care if someone barged into the room and saw them.

'I'm beginning to understand that,' she said, her voice unsteady.

'So we have to think about ways we can make long-distance dating viable.'

'We could just run away—be together somewhere we can just be ourselves, away from expectations,' she said.

'You *know* that's not an option.'

'I so want there to be a chance for *us*,' she said. 'To see if this is more than infatuation.'

'Me too,' he said.

Every minute he spent with her moved him

further away from infatuation into something he couldn't yet put a name to.

'So what do you think are the possible options for us?'

Finn put up his hand to count off the options available to them finger by finger. It was a thing he did. 'Option one—we have a secret no-strings affair. I see you whenever I come to Europe. You sneak down to Sydney when you can.'

'I don't like the idea of sneaky and secretive,' she said. 'And I doubt it would make either of us happy.'

'I would rather be open about our intentions,' he said.

'So let's forget that option,' she said.

'So, option two, we date each other openly as best we can, considering we live on the other side of the world from each other.'

'Which would give you the getting-to-know-each-other period you believe is so important,' she said.

'But it would mean we spend a lot of time apart and we lose our privacy.'

'The media would have a field-day once they got on to it,' she said glumly.

He shuddered 'Horrible. But it would be you they'd be after. I'd get off lightly.'

She shook her head. 'Uh-uh. Once they realise how incredibly handsome you are you'd become a target of the long-distance lens. You've already featured in an *Australian Bachelor Millionaires* article.'

'How did—?'

'I pretty much stalked you for a month after I got back from Sydney. After that… I…it became too heartbreaking.'

'I would have stalked *you* if I'd known who you were,' he said.

She looked so woebegone he could not resist kissing her. Then she snuggled close. He breathed in her scent, already so familiar.

'Still, I like that option,' she said. 'Although the loss of privacy might become an issue.'

'It would become an issue anyway,' he said. 'Because if it worked out between us the next step would be making things more permanent between us.' He put up his hand. 'That doesn't mean I'm proposing. This is a hypothetical discussion, based on the way things work in your family.'

If the day ever came that he asked Natalia to marry him he had strong, traditionally male ideas of how it would happen.

'Of course it's hypothetical,' she said. 'But then—again speaking hypothetically—we would have to face the biggest of the questions. Who lives where?'

'Which means either you live with me in Sydney or I sell my business and live here?'

'That about sums it up,' she said.

He folded his arms across his chest. 'That would be a really big deal for me. To walk away from the company that was my grandparents' would be very hard in terms of family dynamics. I'm very close to my family. It would be difficult for all concerned if I become only an infrequent visitor.'

She crossed her legs, uncrossed them. 'And then there's my side of the story. I'd still remain second in line to the throne. To leave my country would be very difficult. I would almost certainly have to give up my title and all it entails. I was born to be a princess. I know nothing else. I can't earn my own living. The thought is terrifying.'

'It's *all* a bit terrifying,' he said.

She laughed, but there was an edge to her laughter. 'Can you imagine if anyone could overhear us? What a bizarre conversation. To be thinking so far ahead when, as you point out, we hardly know each other.'

'But the unique position we find ourselves in means we have to be aware of all the options.' He paused. 'Which brings us to option three.'

Natalia mock-cringed away from him into the back of the sofa. 'I don't think I'm going to like this one.'

'I sure as hell don't,' he said. 'Option three— total wipe-out, scorched earth, ground zero. We decide that "us" isn't going to work out.' He almost choked on the words. 'We say goodbye—for good this time—and I go back to Australia and wipe you from my life and, in time, from my memory.'

There was a long silence between them. He could hear the old timbers in the chalet shift and settle, the sigh of the wind outside.

'And I stay here and make myself forget I ever met you,' she said finally, her voice wobbling. 'Easier said than done, you realise? I've tried and failed at that already.'

He took a deep steadying breath against the pain that surged through him at the thought of not having her in his life in any way. 'I would have to pull out of my contract with Tristan. Have no communication with Montovia ever again. It would be the only way I could deal with it.'

'Me too. It would be too painful otherwise,' she said slowly, wringing her hands in front of her. 'We…we have to be realistic.'

Realistic? Where did being realistic come in to his hopes for a new life in this fairy tale place full of castles and dungeons and magic, with the most beautiful Princess in the whole wide world?

CHAPTER THIRTEEN

NATALIA WAS REELING from the conversation she'd had with Finn. Yet it was a conversation that had needed to occur. So much for dreams and fantasies and longings…

But there was only so far this common-sense type of discussion could go. She felt propelled by an impulse far more visceral, urgent, intensely personal. Finn was in Montovia for only a little more than twenty-four hours—some of that sleeping time. She intended to claim that sleeping time for herself. To claim *him*.

From where she sat oh-so-safely apart from him on the sofa she faced him. They had been speaking in hushed tones. Now she spoke in a normal, conversational tone, using words that wouldn't matter if anyone overheard.

'Thank you, Finn. That's been a most interesting conversation. You've given me food for thought.' For all Finn had urged her to take the reins, she still felt she needed to work within the rules.

He sat up straighter, frowned at her sudden change of direction. 'Huh…?'

She got up from the sofa. Finn immediately did so too. She was wearing flats and he towered above her. Again she was struck by how handsome he was, dressed all in black, with his black hair and the vibrant green of his eyes, those sharp cheekbones, his fabulous body... He was the most gorgeous man she had ever met. No other man could ever match him.

And not just in looks. Enjoying a man's company as she enjoyed Finn's was a revelation. Business meetings became exciting when he took part. She had wanted him from the moment she had first seen him. She wanted him now. If he left tomorrow and it didn't work out she wanted no regrets.

She held out her hand for a formal handshake. 'Breakfast is in the same room as dinner, starting at seven. We have an eleven o'clock meeting. An early start would be a good idea.'

He took her hand in his firm, warm grip for the politely requisite time before releasing it. 'Yes...' he said, sounding puzzled.

She leaned forward momentarily, to whisper in his ear. 'Don't lock your bedroom door. I'll see you in ten minutes.' Then, in her normal voice, 'Goodnight.'

He grinned and winked at her. He *winked*. The Princess of Montovia wasn't used to being winked at and she loved it.

'Thank you again for your hospitality,' he said, very formally. 'Goodnight.'

She was conscious of his gaze upon her as she left the room. Her first impulse was to race to her bedroom. The faster she showered and changed, the faster she could be back with Finn. But she needed to act normally—not to draw attention to herself if anyone were to see her. All her life she had had to be aware of the staff who shared the royal family's personal space. For most of her waking hours she was observed, one way or another.

She forced herself to walk sedately to her bedroom.

Ten minutes later she emerged, enveloped in the luxurious Italian designer dressing gown she kept at the chalet and toasty Australian wool slippers that had been a gift from Gemma.

Cautiously she crept down the corridor towards Finn's room in the guest wing. She wasn't worried about Marco and Amelie. During dinner Amelie had taken her aside and told her how much she and Marco liked Finn and approved of him.

'Go for it, Natalia,' Amelie had said. 'We had to fight to be together. You might have to as well. Finn is wonderful—he's worth it.'

Encountering Hanna or Bernard would be a different story. They would consider themselves dutybound to report to the Queen what they would see as a breach of royal morality. She was twenty-seven, for heaven's sake, not seventeen. It was

about time she took charge of her own future—
the first step having been her trip to Sydney.

She reached Finn's room without mishap, to
find the door slightly ajar. She tapped so lightly
she thought he might not hear it. But he was there
within seconds. She gasped at the sight of him in
black silk pyjamas with a fine grey stripe. They
showcased his broad shoulders, his lean, muscular body. He was as covered up as if he were in
trousers and a long-sleeved shirt, but somehow
the pyjamas seemed so much more intimate. He
was beautiful in an intensely masculine way.

Without a word, he took her by the hand and
drew her into the room, then locked the door behind her. With a deep murmur of pleasure, he
drew her into his arms and kissed her.

'This is nice,' he said, his voice deep and husky,
when they came up for breath. 'I missed you.
Even for ten minutes I missed you.'

'I missed you too.' Her voice hitched. 'I… I
don't know how I'll bear it when you leave tomorrow.'

'Me neither. As you know, tomorrow I fly to
Dublin with Franz, your master chocolatier, to
meet my contact from the distillery and discuss
the potential for a Montovian chocolate liqueur.
Then I'm scheduled for meetings in London for
three days before flying back to Sydney. Perhaps
you could meet me in London?'

She shook her head. 'I can't. That would be such a red flag to my parents, and I'd rather keep them out of it until we know how it works out for us. Trust me—they will know your schedule and they'll put two and two together very quickly. To my knowledge, they're not aware there is anything between us…although my mother is suspicious.'

'Why is she suspicious? We have given her no cause—'

'She saw the way we were looking at each other at the soirée and drew her own conclusions.'

'Like I'm looking at you now, wondering what you have on under that dressing gown?' His eyes narrowed, gleaming with sensual intent.

'If you'd looked at me like that my mother would have had you evicted from the soirée.'

'And you?'

'I would have gone with you and dragged you back to my apartment.' She reached up to kiss him. 'I'll tell you later what I would have done to you,' she said, her voice laden with promise.

He gave a sensuous growl that both made her smile and sent desire rippling through her.

'I'll look forward to that,' he said. He held her close. 'But in the meantime we continue to keep under the Queen's radar.'

'That's the plan. We need to keep it that way while we figure out how we…*if* we can be together. I don't want my every move to be scrutinised until we invite it. It breaks my heart to say it, because I would love to meet you there, but no London visit for me.'

'Or Dublin or Sydney?'

'Sadly, no.'

He sighed, and she sensed his despair was as deep as hers.

'I won't be able to get back here to see you for another two weeks.' He frowned. 'The dreaded long-distance.'

'I know. I'm dreading it too—which is why I want to make the most of the hours we have left. We don't have much time to take up where we left off in Sydney.' She looked into his eyes. 'And that starts with you helping me out of this dressing gown.'

'Happy to oblige,' he said, his voice husky.

She noticed his hands weren't quite steady as he undid the tie, but they were sure and strong as he pushed the dressing gown off her shoulders, and they felt so good on her bare skin. The dressing gown slid to the floor. She was so new to this. A novice at being naughty.

What next?

She stood proud, wearing only pink lace bra and panties—the same kind as she'd worn in Sydney—and waited for his reaction. Would he notice she wasn't as curvy as she'd been before?

She was not disappointed by his reaction.

'Natalia...' he breathed, his eyes raking over her, gleaming with hunger and admiration. 'I can't believe you wore pink lace. That has figured in my fantasies for three months. You're incredible.'

She was so sure that this was what she wanted—that *he* was what she wanted.

'Not as incredible as you,' she said.

From somewhere came the skill to unfasten his buttons, slide her hands greedily over his chest, revelling in the smoothness of his skin over hard muscle. Such a beautiful man.

'I won't stop you tonight,' she said.

He stilled. 'Are you sure it's what you want?'

'I'm sure. I've thought about it. It's what I want. Is that consent enough for you?'

His hands gripped her upper arms. 'I want you—more than you can imagine. It's just I'm not sure it's right for you just now. The risks and consequences are still the same. If your virginity is such a big deal you were right to be cautious before.' He groaned. 'I must be crazy, holding back. Because there is nothing—absolutely nothing—I want more than to make love with you right now.'

'To be my tutor in living dangerously?' she murmured.

He smiled. 'I'm not convinced you need a tutor in lovemaking. I suspect you'll have things to teach *me*. You're a sensual sensation just waiting to be unleashed.'

'Really?' she said, thrilled at the prospect.

'Oh, yes. The thing is, it's not about me being the tutor and you being the pupil. It's about learning what pleases both yourself and your partner.'

'Like a...like a two-way learning process?' she said breathlessly.

'Exactly.'

He kissed her again, sliding his tongue between her lips, demanding and getting her response before he kissed a trail down her throat to the edge of her bra until she was melting with want.

'The thing is—though it's killing me to say it—I'm going to have to be the responsible one here. There are other ways—exciting ways—for me to please you and you to please me. I'm sure you know about them.'

'I... I haven't done them,' she said, excited in spite of herself.

'Did you know Tristan wanted you to act as my guide because the last time he'd seen you laugh was dancing with me at the wedding?' he asked.

'I didn't know that.'

With two fingers he tilted her chin up so she would look directly into his face. 'In these last few days I've made you laugh many times.'

'Yes,' she said. 'The dark cloud has lifted from me.'

'I've made you laugh...but I can also make you

whimper with want, moan with pleasure, cry out in ecstasy, and then beg me to do it all again.'

She caught her breath as her heart started to hammer and she throbbed in those places she hadn't known could throb until she'd met Finn.

'Can you?' she choked out.

'Oh, yes,' he said, stroking down the side of her breast, and along her waist. 'And that's exactly what I intend to do—starting right now. But you will leave this room still a virgin. I will not have dishonoured you. I hope you will lose your virginity with me when we make a decision about where we're going. But in the meantime you will in all conscience have done your duty to maintain what seems so important in your world.'

'But I—'

He slid his hand towards the edge of her panties.

'*Oh!*'

So that was what a whimper of want felt like.

'Do you want to talk some more? Or shall we take up where we left off three months ago and I'll pick you up and carry you to the bed?'

'The bed. *Please*. The bed.'

Natalia didn't know how much later it was when she woke in Finn's bed. She was lying naked next to him, her head resting on his shoulder, his arm encircling her and holding her tight. *Heaven*. She breathed in the scent of him. The scent of *them*. She felt relaxed to bonelessness after her initiation into the pleasures a woman could both take and give without technically losing her virginity. Never had she dreamed she could be so uninhibited.

She lay next to him, savouring his nearness, thinking. Thinking about Finn, about how unfulfilling her life had been until he'd reappeared in it.

What was the time? How much longer did she have left with him? *Her man.* Privately, that was how she thought of him.

It was still dark. But the nights were getting long at this time of year. She couldn't risk being caught in Finn's bedroom.

Not wanting to wake him, she gently raised herself up on her elbow, looked across at the clock on the nightstand. It glowed in the intense darkness that was night at the chalet, without street lighting or any other buildings. It was not yet three a.m. There was still time.

Still time for *more*.

Everything she'd done with Finn had been intensely exciting and satisfying. But it wasn't enough. She still wanted him.

Her movement must have woken him. He stirred. 'Natalia…' he murmured. 'You're here.'

The joy and pleasure in his voice both thrilled and moved her. He turned, reached out for her.

'You're not going yet?'

Her eyes were getting used to the dark and she could see his face. His handsome, handsome face that had become so dear—so *beloved*—so quickly.

He was the one.

'No, I'm not going.' She reached out with newly confident hands to caress him, revelling in the feel of his body. 'I want you to make love to me, Finn. All the way.'

'But we agreed not to—'

'You were doing the honourable thing, and I appreciate your thoughtfulness more than I can say.'

'Not quite so honourable,' he said 'More trying to be sensible. More trying to...to protect you.'

'I'm frightened, you see,' she said, with a little shiver that had nothing to do with the cold.

'Frightened? There's no need to be—'

She took his hand. 'Not about that. I'm not at *all* frightened about that.'

She dropped a kiss on his hand.

'It's the rest of it. Earlier, on the sofa, when we were discussing our options, I felt so brave—so confident that with you by my side I could reach out and take what I wanted. But in the dark I don't feel so brave. It's difficult to be both a Montovian princess and a feminist, but I do my best. However, it seems to me that when there are decisions to be made it's most often the woman who has to uproot her life. It would most likely be me who'd have change countries. I'm torn. I'm aching to be with you, but I also want to do my duty to my country and to my parents. They have lost one child already and they'd think that me going to Australia would be losing another.'

'I understand,' he said. He picked up a lock of her hair and wound it around his finger, as if binding her to him.

'And, while option two beckons so enticingly, I have to prepare my heart for the fact that option three might be the forerunner. If that's our option, and we have to say goodbye, I want to have been with you in every sense.'

She shifted so she could look right into his face, amazed at how unselfconscious she was about being naked with him.

'You're the one, Finn. No matter how things work out with us, you're the only man I've ever wanted—the only man I have ever imagined I could care for. Please make love to me. Give me memories, if nothing else, that I can carry with me no matter where life might take me.'

'Natalia...' Her name seemed wrenched out of him in a harsh, heartrending sob as he gathered her into his arms.

CHAPTER FOURTEEN

BREAKFAST AT THE chalet early the next morning was a subdued event. Amelie wasn't present because she wasn't feeling well. Morning sickness, Natalia suspected. For the first time in her life, she had a flash of concern for herself—what if she was pregnant? She dismissed the thought—Finn had been meticulous about protection. But then she allowed herself the momentary indulgence of wondering what a child of theirs might be like—almost certainly dark-haired, smart, attractive…

She cast a quick, surreptitious look over to Finn. He seemed sombre, with dark circles under his eyes. Neither of them had got more than a few hours' sleep. They'd found better ways to use their time rather than waste it on sleeping.

The intimacy they'd shared had gone beyond the physical. They'd both been in tears when they'd had to say goodbye in the last private moments they would share until heaven knew when. She had never felt sadder than when she'd sneaked out of his room just before dawn.

She'd felt awkward when she'd got to the breakfast table, to find Finn already there making polite conversation with Marco. Had Marco guessed she'd spent the night with Finn? The only evidence was a slight beard rash, but she'd covered that with make-up.

She longed to seat herself next to Finn—her lover!—as close as she possibly could. But that was out of the question. Instead she acted the gracious hostess to both Finn and Marco.

She gagged at the thought of eating—not the delicious bread rolls Hanna had baked fresh, not Matteo's fabulous cheese or even the finely sliced ham and fresh fruit. Black coffee was all she could tolerate. She was too miserable at the prospect of Finn leaving in just a few hours.

She was about to ask Finn and Marco for the umpteenth time if there was anything else they needed, when she looked up to see big fat snowflakes drifting past the window. She alerted the others.

'The first snow!'

She'd never lost the excitement of the first fall, but she wasn't always at the chalet to see it. Was it an omen that perhaps—just perhaps—things might work out for her and Finn?

With Marco predicting the possibilities of skiable snow, and Finn saying snow was a novelty for a Sydney boy, any awkwardness was smoothed over. And the snowfall propelled her and Finn to start their journey back to the palace straight away, as their driver was worried that the roads might be affected.

They needed to be back in plenty of time for their meeting with the Chamber of Commerce.

She and Finn passed their journey back to the palace in much the way they had the journey to the chalet. The only difference was that Finn spent quite some time on his cell phone, for which he apologised.

'I have to check all is okay with my meetings in Dublin and London.' He leaned over to her. 'I'm glad we've got one more business meeting together.'

'Even if it's likely to be the stuffiest,' she said.

'It's a way to extend our time together for as long as possible. No meeting could possibly be stuffy with you chairing it.'

'Thank you,' she said, aching to touch him— even put her hand on his arm—but knowing it would not be wise. She mustn't risk any hint of scandal—not when they had been so discreet.

Finn was proud of the way Natalia conducted herself at the meeting later that morning. The men and women of the Chamber of Commerce were delighted that their Princess was taking an active interest in local businesses, and Tristan and his savvy sister—Gemma was again absent—worked well together. She would be an asset to any business. To any country.

To him.

It was a kind of torture to play the polite visitor when Natalia was in the room and all he wanted to do was be by her side, claiming her as his own. But he was just a guy from Australia, whose interest lay in the gourmet foods he could import at a profit into his country on the other side of the world.

He was very aware of how deep the roots of this country went. How old the traditions of the people were. How conservative their customs. To uproot Natalia might not be the best option for her.

His grandparents were great gardeners. He knew from working with them that sometimes a plant uprooted from a particular type of soil did not transplant successfully, but rather withered and died. Natalia was the most beautiful flower, adapted to thrive in this fantasy land of castles and dungeons and family retainers. Sydney was an altogether brasher place, and tough in its own way.

Natalia smiled at him from across the room. To chat about chocolate and cheese with her, without acknowledging that she had been in his bed last night, was excruciating.

What he felt for her was so much more than infatuation. It had been from the get-go. He realised that now. Everything about Natalia felt so right, and just her smile sent his heart soaring to heaven. It had nothing to do with her being a princess, and everything to do with her being the perfect woman for him. Yet there were very real obstacles to be overcome.

He *had* to make option two work. In the next two weeks away from her, he would come up with a plan.

At the end of the meeting he shook hands with her in a formal goodbye that tore him apart. He could tell from the almost imperceptible quiver of her lower lip that she was finding it equally torturous. How quickly he'd learned to read her.

As he made his way to the official car that was taking him and the master chocolatier to the airport, and thence to Dublin, he found every excuse to turn back and see ever-diminishing last glimpses of her.

He had a horrible fear that her family would try to make sure he never saw her again. But he would never let that happen.

That afternoon, alone in her apartment, Natalia missed Finn so desperately it physically hurt. She literally could not think of anything else but him.

She had been premature in believing the dark cloud of gloom that had hung over her for so long had dissipated. It had eased. But it was still like a grey fog that strangled the vitality from her, misted her vision of any hope for the future.

He had gone.

The meeting with the Chamber of Commerce that morning had concluded only too quickly After she'd waved Finn goodbye, with the perfectly calibrated royal wave she had been trained to do from a little girl, she'd had a quick chat with Tristan to review the other meetings she'd had with Finn. Her brother seemed to have a high opinion of Finn, and she had sensed Tristan could become an ally if she ever had to fight for her right to be with a man her parents considered unsuitable.

She had to gather her allies. And Tristan had already fought and won his own battle with Montovian tradition.

After her exchange with Tristan she had pleaded a headache and headed for her apartment in the palace. The perfectly decorated apartment that felt suddenly as lonely as if she were in exile.

Despite thoughts of Finn and their options churning through her brain, she decided to try and sleep, fully clothed on her bed. After all, she had had virtually no sleep the night before. But before she was overwhelmed by drowsiness she phoned through to her mother's private secretary and booked an appointment with the Queen for the following morning.

She was pretty sure she knew what she had to do.

At some stage she awoke and reached out for

Finn—only to find cold, empty sheets. Even after one night of sleeping in his arms she knew she wanted him always there—in her bed, by her side, sharing her life. Being with Finn had become more important than anything. This was—at last—love. That elusive emotion she'd feared she might never find. She just hoped—prayed—that Finn felt it too. Because she could never settle for less than his whole-hearted love in return.

Holding that thought, she got up and showered, changed and climbed back into bed.

But sleep didn't come easily, and it was late by the time she drifted off again.

She was woken by the sound of her phone, saw it was still early, reached out to her nightstand, fumbled for the phone and looked for the caller ID.

Finn!

She was immediately awake. Then she burst into tears at the sound of his voice.

'Hey, what's going on?' he said. 'Are those tears I hear?'

She sniffed. 'No. Yes. I was just…overwhelmed to hear your voice. I… I think I had a deep fear I might never talk to you again.'

'That's not going to happen. We're talking now, aren't we? And we need to talk some more.'

'Where are you? In Dublin? London?'

'I'm here. In Montovia.'

She thought she was hearing things. 'At the palace?'

'I didn't think I should storm the walls and come and find you,' he said, in that laconic manner she liked so much. 'I'm at the tea room with the chocolate in the old town. Can you meet me here?'

'Now?'

'If a princess is *allowed* to do such an ordinary thing as meet a man for coffee.'

'This isn't a dream?'

'No.'

'Then the answer is yes!'

Fired with sudden energy, she quickly fixed her hair and applied make-up with hands that trembled with excitement. No matter how desperate she was to see Finn, the Princess of Montovia did *not* go outside the palace looking less than her best.

She threw on skinny black trousers, a tight black cashmere turtleneck, black boots with a heel that could handle cobblestones, and a gorgeous loose-weave wool short coat in different shades of pink that she'd been too depressed to wear after she'd bought it. Contemporary pink ruby earrings and a bracelet completed the look.

She booked a palace car to take her down to the old town and then ran from her apartment— something that really wasn't done in the corridors of the royal palace of Montovia.

CHAPTER FIFTEEN

NATALIA STILL WASN'T quite sure that Finn's call hadn't been a dream—a manifestation of her longing for him. But there he was, sitting at the most private table available at the tea room. He rose to greet her, darkly handsome in a superbly tailored business suit. Joy bubbled up inside her.

She forced herself to walk to him at a suitably sedate pace, when really she wanted to run and fling herself into his arms. She greeted him with a businesslike handshake, then sat down opposite him. This was one place where she would be observed and her behaviour noted by the townsfolk.

He'd ordered her the hot chocolate she'd been enjoying here since she was a child. He had a coffee in front of him—short and black. He offered her a chocolate croissant, but she declined.

'It's so good to see you,' he said, his voice hushed.

Hopefully there was enough clatter from the other tables to mask their conversation.

'Oh, Finn, I can't tell you how amazing it is to see you. I... I think my heart is literally jumping for joy. But what are you doing here? How...? Why...?'

'I cancelled my meetings in London, postponed my flight back to Sydney and flew back here from Dublin after the meeting. I stayed last night in a small hotel near the clock tower. Not that I slept.'

'Why didn't you tell me?'

'It was late when I got in. Besides, I needed some time to plan my strategy.' He leaned across the table towards her, his eyes intense. 'You see, beautiful, wonderful, perfect Natalia, I realised nothing was more important in my life than you. *Nothing.*'

'Oh, Finn, I feel the same.'

Her heart soared with the knowledge that he cared for her too. She ached to kiss him, but she knew they had an audience. A discreet, quiet audience, but an audience just the same.

'I wanted a plan for how to put option two into action. But option two without the separation, the long-distance angst. I decided I would come here to live. Not permanently. I thought three months…on a tourist visa. I could find an apartment here in the old town, so I would be near to you in the castle. As long as it had good Wi-Fi, I could work remotely. Then, as we discussed, we could start dating. Three months should give us time to get to know each other better.'

He looked very pleased with himself.

Her heart soared. 'But, Finn, I—'

He put up his hand to stop her. 'Hear me out.

I can afford to ease off the pedal on my business for a few months. I've thought about what you said about being frightened. I realised I was scared too—of leaving behind my country and people I love to be a foreigner in a strange land.'

'It *is* scary,' she said.

'But that's exactly what my family did. My father left Ireland for a better life than on the small farm where he grew up. When my great-grandparents emigrated to Australia they left everything—everyone—for the chance of a better life. My Chinese great-grandparents were fleeing persecution…my Italian great-grandparents were fleeing poverty. In their day, there were only letters that took weeks to be delivered to communicate with the loved ones they'd left behind. My Chinese great-grandparents never saw their parents again. My grandparents had to fight prejudice and racism to be together and become the Romeo and Juliet of their suburb. *That's* the background I come from. Why shouldn't I be prepared to emigrate to build a life with you? I want to give it a trial for three months. That is if it's what you want too.'

Natalia laughed a laugh that she knew was tinged with hysteria. 'But I had the same idea. I decided we should try option two without all the long-distance to-ing and fro-ing by me living in Sydney for a while.'

'What?'

'Yes!' She lowered her voice. 'The plan I came up with was that I would come and live in Sydney for six months, so we could spend time together and get to know each other better. But perhaps three months might be more feasible. I would take a sabbatical from some of my charity commitments and work online for the auctions. I have good people to help here while I'm away. I thought of leasing an apartment near where Eliza and Jake live. You wouldn't be far. Perhaps I could meet your family, too? But the idea is to be *near* you, Finn. After our time in the chalet I cannot bear the thought of being parted from you again.'

'I hated being apart from you just that one night.'

He laughed, and she loved the edge of incredulous delight in his laughter.

'I can't believe we independently came up with two versions of the same solution at the same time.'

'Perhaps we can do both,' she said.

'Why not? I'll live in Montovia near you for three months…' he said.

'Then I'll move to Sydney for three months to be with you. I would *love* that. I was going to call you this morning to see what you thought of my idea.'

'And now I'm here to talk to you in person, because I couldn't stay away from you.'

'I've booked a meeting with my mother this morning, to tell her of my plans. But I'll go with you to Sydney anyway—even if she doesn't approve.' She paused. 'Your approval is all I need, Finn.'

'You have it wholeheartedly. We will make the decisions that affect our lives. And, while I'm certain I'll enjoy my three months living here near you, I will love having you in Sydney. I know my family will welcome you with open arms.'

'Oh, Finn, this is just wonderful!'

He leaned across the table and kissed her, his lips firm and possessive on hers. The kiss was short and sweet and utterly heartfelt.

And greeted by a chorus of applause and bravos.

Natalia broke away from the kiss and saw the smiling face of the tea room proprietor—a jovial, elderly man who had known her since she was a child. Everyone else in the shop would know who she was too, and about her history of turning down proposal after proposal, but all she saw were kind faces and goodwill.

She smiled back, unable to contain her joy that Finn was in her life and they could be open about what they meant to each other.

The alarm on her watch went off. *'Ack!* I'm

meeting with my mother in twenty minutes. I've got to go—try and head her off before the news breaks that the Princess was seen kissing a handsome foreigner in the chocolate shop.'

'I'm coming too. We'll face her together. Let's start as we mean to continue—as a couple.'

They left the tea room to further applause, and headed for Natalia's car and driver.

'Wait,' Finn said. 'I have a suggestion. Rather than confronting the Queen with a *fait accompli*, why don't we ask her advice on how we can make it work?'

'Good idea,' Natalia said. '*Excellent* idea. You might end up a Montovian diplomat yet.'

Natalia was glad they'd agreed on Finn's strategy. When they entered the Queen's office she could tell by her mother's frosty expression that the news from the tea room had already reached her.

Her mother sat behind her ornate antique desk. She did not offer Natalia and Finn a chair, but rather let them stand. Finn gave a deep bow to the Queen, as Natalia had coached him. He did an excellent job. It was as if he were born to it.

'Your Majesty, Natalia and I beg your forgiveness for our indiscreet behaviour in the tea room.'

'We're in a relationship, Mother,' Natalie said. 'We couldn't help it. By the time you told me to "nip it in the bud" it was too late. This morning I was so happy I forgot I shouldn't be kissing Finn in public. Please take me off the royal matchmaking list. From now on I'm only dating Finn.'

'Where do you think this will take you?' said the Queen.

'To a future together, I hope,' she said.

She cast a sideways glance at Finn, who nodded.

Finn took Natalia's hand. 'We need to spend more time together, Your Majesty,' he said. 'However, that is complicated by the fact that we live in different countries on different sides of the world.'

'So I'm going to spend three months in Sydney with Finn,' Natalia blurted out.

So much for diplomacy. But she had lived by the royal rules for so long—she needed to make a strong statement about how now she wanted to live her life her own way.

With Finn.

'But first I plan to spend three months in Montovia, Your Majesty,' he said. 'We are seeking your advice on how we can best accomplish this. And of course Natalia will want to discuss with you the logistics of her taking some time to spend in Sydney.'

Natalia marvelled at how Finn had got the tone of his speech just right.

'Do you intend to live together?' asked the Queen.

'We intend to maintain separate residences,' he said. 'In both Montovia and Sydney. For three months in each country.'

'The King and I have given this matter considerable thought over the last few days.'

'What matter?' asked Natalia. 'Me and Finn? Mother, what do you mean, you and Father have been discussing it for the last few days? We have only just realised ourselves that we want to be together.'

The Queen quoted a Montovian saying that pretty much translated as telling them that she hadn't come down in the last shower. 'I saw how miserable you were when you got back from Sydney. How that misery lifted once this young man appeared at the palace.'

'Oh…' Natalia said, exchanging a glance with Finn.

'And if you make your living arrangements more permanent, where do you plan to live?'

'I would live wherever is best for Natalia,' Finn said.

'I realise that as second in line to the throne I am obliged to live here,' Natalia said.

She looked around her mother's ornate and exquisitely decorated office and thought about how much she loved the palace and the castle and being Princess of Montovia.

'Or I can make the choice to renounce my title.'

It hurt even to say the words. Renouncing her title would mean alienation from the family she loved. But she wanted to be with Finn—whatever the cost.

The Queen smiled the stiff smile that came from her regular wrinkle-fighting injections. 'Recent events have taken the pressure off you in that regard. Gemma is pregnant—'

Natalia clapped her hands together. 'I *knew* it. How wonderful! I'm so thrilled—'

Her mother raised her hand imperiously. 'Please let me continue, Natalia.'

'Yes, Mother.'

'Gemma is pregnant with twins. A boy and a girl. She has held off from sharing the news because there is a greater risk of complication with twins. However, her consultant has given her the all-clear to make the announcement. What this means for you is that once the twins are born you will go from being second in line to the throne to fourth. I know that will make you happy.'

'Yes, Mother it does.' She felt as though the enormous weight that had been crushing her since Carl's death had been lifted. 'I am delighted for Gemma and Tristan about the twins. And for you and Father. Not just because there will be new heirs, but new grandchildren.'

'It is happy news,' the Queen said.

Still there was the sadness of loss in her eyes,

but there was also joyful anticipation of new life. The new babies would do much to heal the wounds in her family that had made Natalia's life so constricted.

'The best kind of happy news,' Natalia said.

The Queen continued. 'You should know that if you and Finn decide to marry you have our permission.'

Was she hearing things?

'Really?'

'I told you—I want you to be happy. It is not just the news about the twins that has prompted our decision. However, there is a condition. If you decide to make your home in Australia we would require you to make regular return trips home to Montovia.'

'To fulfil my royal duties?'

'To see your mother and father. We would miss you, my darling.'

After they'd left the Queen's office Finn asked Natalia to take him up to the arched lookouts, with their magnificent view across the lake.

'We need some privacy and a place to think,' he explained.

As they walked up the steps and along the battlements, holding hands, he marvelled to himself at how the castle, the town, the country that had seemed like a movie set, populated by witches and wizards, was now beginning to seem like home. Because it was Natalia's home.

Perhaps one day she would feel the same about the view from the veranda of his house across to the Sydney Harbour Bridge and the Opera House.

When they reached the middle archway he put his arm around her and pulled her close. In silence, they both looked out at the view. He wondered if Natalia, as he was, was taking some quiet time to process that astonishing pronouncement by the Queen—that she and the King gave their permission for him to marry her daughter.

She wasn't wearing a hat, and a teasing chilly breeze was lifting her hair and blowing it across her face. He turned her to him and gently pushed her hair back into place. Then he cradled her chin in his hands and tilted her face upwards, so he could look into her eyes.

'I love you, Natalia,' he said, his voice hoarse with emotion. 'I already know all I need to know about you and I know I could not imagine a life without you in it.'

His beautiful princess closed her eyes and then opened them again, as if scarcely able to believe she was here with him. Her mouth curved in the most joyous of smiles. 'Oh, Finn, I love you too. I think I fell in love with you that first day in Sydney. Only because I've never been in love before I didn't recognise it.'

'The whole time we've been discussing our three-month plan for option two I've been thinking we don't really need to spend time dating. I don't want to live apart from you. I love you. I adore you. I want to marry you, and have children with you, and wake up every morning to your face on my pillow.'

'Oh, Finn…' She sighed. 'That sounds like heaven.'

He reached into the inner pocket of his jacket and pulled out a small velvet covered box. 'Natalia, will you do me the honour of becoming my wife? I love you and I want to honour and cherish you for the rest of our lives—not because you're a princess, but because you're the most wonderful woman ever put on this earth.'

She put her hand to her heart, seeming almost too overcome to speak. But she managed to choke out some words. 'Yes, Finn—yes. I love you and I want to honour and cherish you too. More than anything I want to be your wife.'

His wife. Two such wonderful words.

He took her left hand and slid onto the third finger an engagement ring magnificent in its simplicity—a large, oval cut white diamond on a narrow platinum band. He'd guessed the size just right.

She held out her hand and splayed her fingers to admire the ring as its facets caught the light and glistened with tiny rainbows. 'It's beautiful. I love it. But how—?'

'My cousin in Dublin directed me to the best jeweller in town. I didn't think I'd get a chance to give it to you quite so soon.'

He kissed her long and sweet and tenderly.

Natalia pulled away from his kiss and leaned back against the circle of his arms. 'You realise this is where Tristan proposed to Gemma?'

'I do. I know how important tradition is to the older Montovians. Why not start some traditions for our generation?'

'When we marry you'll be a Montovian too. You become a citizen on marriage.'

'I'd like us to marry as soon as we can. But I'd still like to do the three months in each country. What do you think?'

'Me too. Only, because we're engaged, we might actually be able to live together. And, in light of your proposal, maybe I should come to Australia first, so we can be here in Montovia for the three months before the wedding.'

'I thought something simple, private...'

She gave a snort of most un-princess-like laughter.

'*Simple?* I am Princess of Montovia and my parents' only daughter. I'm afraid we can't have "simple". Don't even try to fight for it. We'll have a spectacular royal wedding in our beautiful cathedral with all the ceremonial bling. Nothing less.'

Finn realised that his private life out of the spotlight was about to come to a screeching halt. But with Natalia by his side he didn't care nearly as much as he'd thought he might.

'My family will love a big cathedral wedding,' he said. 'What about that glass carriage drawn by white horses?'

He was joking. Natalia was not.

'The horses—yes; the glass carriage—not possible. But there *is* a royal landau. It's an open carriage, so that means a spring wedding.'

'Six months away? Perfect timing. At the end of our time getting to know each other better.'

'I'm going to enjoy every second of it,' she said.

'We have a lifetime together ahead for us, my beautiful wife-to-be,' said Finn, drawing her into his arms.

He couldn't imagine ever feeling happier than he did at this moment, but he suspected that being married to Natalia would mean happiness compounding upon happiness.

EPILOGUE

Six months later

NATALIA COULD FEEL the goodwill emanating from the Montovian citizens who crowded the cathedral square, hoping to catch a glimpse of their Princess in her wedding dress as she alighted from the sleek black limousine with her father King Gerard. There was a media contingent too, with cameras at the ready, so sizeable it had to be kept in check by members of the royal family's personal guard.

There was intense interest in her love story with Finn all around the world. A beautiful European princess marrying a handsome Australian commoner was story enough. But the 'Secret Princess' angle was what had sent their love story viral.

Not long after they had made the formal announcement of their engagement some sharp-eyed person in Eliza's circle had noticed the resemblance blonde wedding guest Natalie Gerard bore to dark-haired Natalia, Princess of Montovia. And when photos of her dancing with Finn at Eliza's wedding were published, Natalia's cover was completely blown.

Now the whole world knew how they had met. But, despite media digging, no scandal had been unearthed. Rather, their story was being celebrated for its heady level of romance.

Natalia alighted from the car, waved to the crowd, then climbed the stairs to the cathedral on her father's arm, her long train trailing behind her.

At the top of the steps her bridesmaids were there to greet her, dressed in exquisite long gowns in gradating tones of pink—Gemma, new mother to the world's most adorable twins, Amelie, heavily pregnant, Finn's beautiful sister Bella, already a dear friend, and three of her close Montovian friends.

They clustered around her to pat her hair into place and adjust the filmy veil that covered her face, anchored by the diamond tiara her great-great-grandmother had worn, before it fell to the hem of her white lace gown. They fussed with her bouquet of indigenous Australian blooms—flannel flowers, white waratah and orchids, airfreighted from Sydney. Then they kissed her for good luck.

Her bridesmaids left her to walk in procession, one by one, down the long, long aisle to the high altar of the cathedral. The same altar where her ancestors, stretching back generation after generation, had wed.

Natalia stood with her father as the organ music swelled and she started her own stately march down the aisle to where Finn waited for her— her husband-to-be. There were gasps of admiration from the congregation as she made her way down the carpet.

She was pleased. She wanted Finn to gasp too. His reaction to how she looked was the only one she cared about. Her dress was made in a similar style to the pink dress she'd worn in Sydney when she'd first met him, only by the original Paris designer, and the silk lace was heavy and luxurious, the design simple in its construction.

Every pew in the cathedral was packed with people who had come to witness her wedding and wish her well. All she could see was a mass of smiling faces.

As she got to the first few rows she recognised her family and friends. The Queen in the ornately carved monarch's pew. Her new family, Finn's parents and his grandparents, whom she already adored. The other Party Queens and their husbands—Eliza holding her baby girl.

And next to Eliza sat her neighbour Kerry, she of the uncannily accurate prediction, who had been high on the invitation list. Her new prediction was for a long and happy life for the bride and groom and their three children yet to be born.

And then there was Finn—her beloved Finn—standing by Tristan, his best man. Her husband-to-be, tall and handsome, in an immaculately tailored morning suit. When she finally reached him, he was obviously too overcome to say anything, but his eyes told her everything she needed to know about how he felt about his bride.

Her father handed her over to the new man in her life and slid back to his pew.

'You are the most beautiful bride I've ever seen,' Finn whispered when he found his words. 'I'm a lucky, lucky man.'

'I'm the lucky one—to have found you,' she whispered back. 'Want to see my "something borrowed"?'

Her 'something old' was the diamond tiara. The 'something new' her gown. The 'something blue' was the sapphire and diamond necklace and earrings gifted to her by her parents.

She held up her right wrist. 'This is my "something borrowed".'

Finn stared at the fine platinum bangle from which dangled the cufflink he had left behind in her hotel room back in Sydney, where it had all started.

'So that's where it went,' he said. 'I was too busy searching for you to look for it.'

'I kept it close to my heart, always hoping I'd see you again,' she whispered.

Every day she fell more and more in love with him.

'We'll never be parted again, I promise you,' he said, taking her hand, drawing her close and facing the archbishop as the ceremony that would make them husband and wife commenced.

After the service had ended—having been conducted in both Montovian and English—Finn sat back in the antique open landau drawn by four perfectly matched white horses that was taking him and his brand-new wife on a ceremonial tour through the ancient cobbled streets of the old town of Montovia. It was a perfect May day.

The narrow thoroughfares were lined with well-wishers waving the Montovian flag, with its emblem of an eagle with a sword in its beak, and the occasional Australian flag. Along with Natalia he waved back, soon losing his self-consciousness at doing such an unaccustomed thing.

Again, he felt as though he'd been plunged into the set of a fantasy movie as the carriage wound its way through the shadow of the ancient castle that stood guard over the town, past the famous medieval clock and the rows of quaint houses that were multiple centuries older than anything in Australia—all to the accompaniment of the glorious chiming of bells from one of the oldest cathedrals in Europe and the cheers of the crowd in a language he was only just beginning to master.

He turned to his bride. 'I love you, Natalia, my wife, for ever and for always,' he said as he kissed her.

The crowd erupted with joyous cheering.

His heart was full of love and gratitude that, as in the best of fantasies, he and his real-life Princess Natalia were being given their very own fairy tale happy-ever-after and beginning their new life together.

* * * * *

If you enjoyed this story,
check out these other great reads
from Kandy Shepherd

Second Chance with the Single Dad
Best Man and the Runaway Bride
Stranded with Her Greek Tycoon
Conveniently Wed to the Greek

All available now!